JUN 0 5 2014

THE SNOW QUEEN

THE SNOW QUEEN

MICHAEL CUNNINGHAM

HARPERCOLLINS*PUBLISHERSLTD*

This book is for Billy Hough

Empty, vast, and cold were the halls of the Snow Queen. The flickering flame of the northern lights could be plainly seen, whether they rose high or low in the heavens, from every part of the castle. In the midst of its empty, endless hall of snow was a frozen lake, broken on its surface into a thousand forms; each piece resembled another, from being in itself perfect as a work of art, and in the centre of this lake sat the Snow Queen, when she was at home. She called the lake "The Mirror of Reason," and said that it was the best, and indeed the only one in the world.

—Hans Christian Andersen, *The Snow Queen*

A Night

A celestial light appeared to Barrett Meeks in the sky over Central Park, four days after Barrett had been mauled, once again, by love. It was by no means his first romantic dropkick, but it was the first to have been conveyed by way of a five-line text, the fifth line of which was a crushingly corporate wish for good luck in the future, followed by three lowercase xxx's.

During the past four days, Barrett had been doing his best to remain undiscouraged by what seemed, lately, to be a series of progressively terse and tepid breakups. In his twenties, love had usually ended in fits of weeping, in shouts loud enough to set off the neighbors' dogs. On one occasion, he and his soon-to-be-ex had fought with their fists (Barrett can still hear the table tipping over, the sound the pepper mill made as it rolled lopsidedly across the floorboards). On another: a shouting match on Barrow Street, a bottle shattered (the words "falling in love" still suggest, to Barrett, green glass shards on a sidewalk under a streetlamp), and the voice of an old woman, neither shrill nor scolding, emanating from some low dark window, saying, simply, "Don't you boys understand that people live here, people are trying to sleep," like the voice of an exhausted mother.

As Barrett moved into his mid-, and then late, thirties, though, the partings increasingly tended to resemble business negotiations. They were not devoid of sorrow and accusation, but they had without question become less hysterical. They'd come to resemble deals and investments that had, unfortunately, gone wrong, despite early promises of solid returns.

This last parting, however, was his first to be conveyed by text, the farewell appearing, uninvited, unanticipated, on a screen no bigger than a bar of hotel soap. *Hi Barrett I guess u know what this is about. Hey we gave it our best shot right?*

Barrett did not, in fact, know what this was about. He got the message, of course—love, and whatever future love implied, had been canceled. But, *I guess u know what this is about?* That had been something like a dermatologist saying, offhandedly, after your annual checkup, *I guess you know that that beauty mark on your cheek, that little chocolate-colored speck that has been referred to, more than once, as an aspect of your general loveliness (who was it who said Marie Antoinette's penciled-on version had been in precisely that spot?), is actually skin cancer.*

Barrett responded initially in kind, by text. An e-mail

seemed elderly, a phone call desperate. So he tapped out, on tiny keys, *Wow this is sudden how bout we talk a little, I'm where I always am. xxx.*

By the end of the second day, Barrett had left two more texts, followed by two voice mails, and had spent most of the second night not leaving a third. By the end of day number three, he had not only received no reply of any kind, but also had begun to realize there would be no reply at all; that the sturdily built, earnest Canadian Ph.D. candidate (psychology, Columbia) with whom he'd shared five months of sex and food and private jokes, the man who'd said "I might actually love you" after Barrett recited Frank O'Hara's "Ave Maria" while they were taking a bath together, the one who'd known the names of the trees when they spent that weekend in the Adirondacks, was simply moving on; that Barrett had been left standing on the platform, wondering how exactly he seemed to have missed his train.

I wish you happiness and luck in the future. xxx.

On the fourth night, Barrett was walking across Central Park, headed home after a dental exam, which struck him on one hand as depressingly commonplace but, on the other, as a demonstration of his fortitude. Go ahead, rid yourself of me in five uninformative and woundingly anonymous lines. (*I'm sorry it just hasn't worked out the way we'd hoped it would, but I know we both tried our best.*) I'm not going to neglect my teeth for you. I'm going to be pleased, pleased and thankful, to know that I don't need a root canal, after all.

Still, the idea that, without having been offered any time to prepare for it, he'd never witness the pure careless loveliness of this young man, who was so much like those lithe, innocent young athletes adoringly painted by Thomas Eakins; the idea that Barrett would never again watch the boy peel his briefs off before bed, never witness his lavish, innocent delight in small satisfactions (a Leonard Cohen mix tape Barrett made for him, called *Why Don't You Just Kill Yourself*; a victory for the Rangers), seemed literally impossible, a violation of love-physics. As did the fact that Barrett would, apparently, never know what it was that had gone so wrong. There had been, during the last month or so, the occasional fight, the awkward lapse in conversation. But Barrett had assumed that the two of them were merely entering the next phase; that their disagreements (Do you think you could try not to be late *some* of the time? Why would you put me down like that in front of my friends?) were signposts of their growing intimacy. He hadn't remotely imagined that one morning he'd check his text messages and find love to have been lost, with approximately the degree of remorse one would feel over the loss of a pair of sunglasses.

On the night of the apparition, Barrett, having been relieved of the threatened root canal, having promised to floss more faithfully, had crossed the Great Lawn and was nearing the floodlit, glacial mass of the Metropolitan Museum. He was crunching over ice-coated silver-gray snow, taking a shortcut to the number 6 train, dripped on by tree branches, glad at least to be going home to Tyler and Beth, glad to have someone waiting for him. He felt numb, as if his whole being had been injected with novocaine. He wondered if he was becoming, at the age of thirty-eight, less a figure of tragic ardency, love's holy fool, and more a middle manager who wrote off one deal (yes, there've been some losses to the company portfolio, but nothing catastrophic) and went on to the next, with renewed if slightly more reasonable

aspirations. He no longer felt inclined to stage a counterat-
tack, to leave hourly voice mails or stand sentry outside his
ex's building, although, ten years ago, that's exactly what
he'd have done: Barrett Meeks, a soldier of love. Now he
could only picture himself as aging and destitute. If he summoned up a show of anger and ardency it would merely be
meant to disguise the fact that he was broke, he was broken,
please, brother, have you got anything you can spare?

Barrett hung his head as he walked through the park,
not from shame but weariness, as if his head had become too
heavy to hold upright. He looked down at the modest blue-
gray puddle of his own shadow, cast by the lampposts onto
the snow. He watched his shadow glide over a pinecone, a
vaguely runic scattering of pine needles, and the wrapper of
an Oh Henry! bar (they still made Oh Henry! bars?) that
rattled by, raggedly silver, windblown.

The miniature groundscape at his feet struck him, rather
suddenly, as too wintery and prosaic to bear. He lifted his
heavy head and looked up.

There it was. A pale aqua light, translucent, a swatch of
veil, star-high, no, lower than the stars, but high, higher than
a spaceship hovering above the treetops. It may or may not
have been slowly unfurling, densest at its center, trailing off
at its edges into lacy spurs and spirals.

Barrett thought that it must be a freakish southerly ap-
pearance of the aurora borealis, not exactly a common sight
over Central Park, but as he stood—a pedestrian in coat and
scarf, saddened and disappointed but still regular as regular,
standing on a stretch of lamp-lit ice—as he looked up at the
light, as he thought it was probably all over the news—as he
wondered whether to stand where he was, privately surprised,

or go running after someone else for corroboration—there were other people, the dark cutouts of them, right there, arrayed across the Great Lawn . . .

In his uncertainty, his immobility, standing stolid in Timberlands, it came to him. He believed—he knew—that as surely as he was looking up at the light, the light was looking back down at him.

No. Not looking. *Apprehending*. As he imagined a whale might apprehend a swimmer, with a grave and regal and utterly unfrightened curiosity.

He felt the light's attention, a tingle that ran through him, a minute electrical buzz; a mild and pleasing voltage that permeated him, warmed him, seemed perhaps ever so slightly to illuminate him, so that he was brighter than he'd been, just a shade or two; phosphorescent, but pinkly so, humanly so, nothing of swamp gas about it, just a gathering of faint blood-light that rose to the surface of his skin.

And then, neither slowly nor quickly, the light dissipated. It waned into a scattering of pale blue sparks that seemed somehow animated, like the playful offspring of a placid and titanic parent. Then they, too, winked out, and the sky was as it had been, as it has always been.

He remained standing for a while, watching the sky as if it were a television screen that had suddenly gone blank and might, just as mysteriously, turn itself on again. The sky, however, continued to offer only its compromised darkness (the lights of New York City gray the nocturnal blackness), and the sparse pinpoints of stars powerful enough to be seen at all. Finally, he continued on his way home, to Beth and Tyler, to the modest comforts of the apartment in Bushwick.

What else, after all, was he supposed to do?

NOVEMBER 2004

It's snowing in Tyler and Beth's bedroom. Flecks of snow—tough little ice balls, more BB than flake, more gray than white in the early morning dimness—swirl onto the floorboards and the foot of the bed.

Tyler awakens from a dream, which dissolves almost entirely, leaving only a sensation of queasy and peevish joy. When he opens his eyes it seems, for a moment, that the skeins of snow blowing around the room are part of his dream, a manifestation of icy and divine mercy. But it is in fact real snow, blowing in through the window he and Beth left open last night.

Beth sleeps curled into the circle of Tyler's arm. He gently disengages himself, gets up to close the window. He walks barefoot across the snow-sparkled floor, doing what needs to be done. This is satisfying. He's the sensible one. In Beth, he has finally found someone more romantically impractical than he. Beth, if she woke, would, in all likelihood, ask him to leave the window open. She'd like the idea of their cramped, crowded little bedroom (the books pile up, and Beth won't shed her habit of bringing home treasures she finds on the streets—the hula-girl lamp that could, in theory, be rewired; the battered leather suitcase; the two spindly, maidenly chairs) as a life-size snow globe.

Tyler shuts the window, with effort. Everything in this apartment is warped. A marble dropped in the middle of the living room would roll right out the front door. As he forces the sash down, a final fury of snow blows in, as if seeking its last chance at . . . what? . . . the annihilating warmth of Tyler and Beth's bedroom, this brief offer of heat and dissolution? . . . As the miniature flurry blasts over him, a cinder blows into his eye; or maybe some obdurate microscopic ice crystal, like the tiniest imaginable sliver of glass. Tyler rubs his eye, can't seem to get at the speck that's embedded itself there. It's as if he's been subjected to a minor mutation; as if the clear speck had attached itself to his cornea, and so he stands with one eye clear and one bleary and watering, watching the snowflakes hurl themselves against the glass. It's barely six o'clock. It's white outside, everywhere. The elderly snow-piles that have been, day after day, plowed to the edges of the next-door parking—that have solidified into miniature gray mountains, touched toxically, here and there, with spangles of soot—are now, for now, alpine, like something out of a Christmas card; or, rather, something out of a Christmas card if you focus tightly, edit out the cocoa-colored, concrete facade of the empty warehouse (upon which the ghost of the word "concrete" is still emblazoned, although grown so faint it's as if the building itself, so long neglected, still insists on announcing its own name) and the still-slumbering street where the neon Q in the LIQUOR sign winks and buzzes like a distress flare. Even in this tawdry cityscape, though—this haunted, half-empty neighborhood, where the burned carcass of an old Buick has remained (strangely pious in its rusted-out, gutted and graffitied, absolute uselessness) for the last year, on the street beneath Tyler's window—there's a gaunt beauty summoned by the pre-dawn light; a sense of compromised but still-living hope. Even in Bushwick. Here's a fall of new snow, serious snow, immaculate, with its hint of benediction, as if some company that delivers hush and accord to the better neighborhoods had gotten the wrong address.

If you live in certain places, in a certain way, you'd better learn to praise the small felicities.

And, living as Tyler does in this place, in this placidly impoverished neighborhood of elderly aluminum siding, of warehouses and parking lots, all utilitarian, all built on the cheap, with its just-barely-managing little businesses and its daunted denizens (Dominicans, mostly, people who went to considerable effort to get here—who had, must have had, higher hopes than those that Bushwick has granted them) trudging dutifully along to or from minimum-wage jobs—as if defeat could no longer be defeated, as if one were lucky to have anything at all. It isn't even particularly dangerous anymore; there is of course the occasional robbery but it seems, for the most part, that even the criminals have lost their ambition. In a place like this, praise is elusive. It's difficult to stand at a window, watching snow feather onto the overflowing garbage cans (the garbage trucks seem to remember, sporadically, unpredictably, that there's garbage to collect here, too) and the cracked cobblestones, without thinking ahead to its devolution into dun-colored sludge, the brown tarns of ankle-deep street-corner puddles upon which cigarette butts and balls of foil gum wrappers (fool's silver) will float.

Tyler should go back to bed. Another interlude of sleep and who knows, he might wake into a world of more advanced, resolute cleanliness, a world wearing a still-heavier white blanket over its bedrock of drudgery and ash.

He's reluctant, however, to leave the window in this condition of sludgy wistfulness. Going back to bed now would be too much like seeing a delicately emotional stage play that comes to neither a tragic nor happy ending, that begins to sputter out until there are no more actors onstage, until the audience realizes that the play must be over, that it's time to get up and leave the theater.

Tyler has promised he'll cut down. He's been good about it, for the past couple of days. But now, right now, it's a minor metaphysical emergency. Beth isn't worse, but she isn't better, either. Knickerbocker Avenue is waiting patiently through its brief interlude of accidental beauty until it can return to the slush and puddle that is its natural state.

All right. This morning, he'll give himself a break. He can re-summon his rigor easily enough. This is only a boost, at a time when a boost is needed.

He goes to the nightstand, takes his vial from the drawer, and sucks up a couple of quick ones.

And here it is. Here's the sting of livingness. He's back

after his nightly voyage of sleep, all clarity and purpose; he's renewed his citizenship in the world of people who strive and connect, people who mean business, people who burn and want, who remember everything, who walk lucid and unafraid.

He returns to the window. If that windblown ice crystal meant to weld itself to his eye, the transformation is already complete; he can see more clearly now with the aid of this minuscule magnifying mirror . . .

Here's Knickerbocker Avenue again, and, yes, it will soon return to its ongoing condition of anywhereness, it's not as if Tyler has forgotten that, but the grimy impending future doesn't matter, in very much the way Beth says that morphine doesn't eradicate the pain but puts it aside, renders it unimportant, a sideshow curiosity, mortifying (See the Snake Boy! See the Bearded Lady!) but remote and, of course, a hoax, just spirit gum and latex.

Tyler's own, lesser pain, the dampness of his inner workings, all those wires that hiss and spark in his brain, has been snapped dry by the coke. A moment ago, he was fuzzed out and mordant, but now—quick suck of harsh magic—he's all acuity and verve. He's shed his own costume, and the true suit of himself fits him perfectly. Tyler is a one-man audience, standing naked at a window at the start of the twenty-first century, with hope clattering in his rib cage. It seems possible that all the surprises (he didn't exactly plan on being an unknown musician at forty-three, living in eroticized chastity with his dying girlfriend and his younger brother, who has turned, by slow degrees, from a young wizard into a tired middle-aged magician, summoning doves out of a hat for the ten thousandth time) have been part of an inscrutable effort, too immense to see; some accumulation of lost chances and canceled plans and girls who were almost but not quite, all of which seemed random at the time but have brought him here, to this window, to his difficult but interesting life, his bulldoggish loves, his still-taut belly (the drugs help) and jut of dick (his own) as the Republicans are about to go down and a new world, cold and clean, is set to begin.

Tyler will get a rag and wipe the melted snow off the floorboards. He will take care of it. He will adore Beth and Barrett with more purity. He will gather and procure, take on an extra shift at the bar, praise the snow and all it touches. He will get them out of this grim apartment, sing ferociously into the heart of the world, find an agent, stitch it all together, remember to soak the beans for cassoulet, get Beth to chemo on time, do less coke and cut out Dilaudid entirely, finally finish reading *The Scarlet and the Black*. He will hold Beth and Barrett, console them, remind them of how little there is to worry about, feed them, tell them the stories that render them that much more visible to themselves.

Outside, the snow shifts with a shift in the wind, and it seems as if some benign force, some vast invisible watcher, has known what Tyler wanted, the moment before he knew it himself—a sudden animation, a change, the gentle steady snowfall taken up and turned into fluttering sheets, an airy map of the wind currents; and yes—are you ready, Tyler?— it's time to release the pigeons, five of them, from the liquor store roof, time to set them aflight and then (are you watching?) turn them, silvered by early light, counter to the wind-blown flakes, sail them effortlessly west into the agitated air that's blowing the snow toward the East River (where barges will be plowing, whitened like ships of ice, through the choppy water); and yes, right, a moment later it's time to turn the streetlights off and, simultaneously, bring a truck around the corner of Rock Street, its headlights still on and its flat silver top blinking little warning lights, garnet and ruby, that's perfect, that's amazing, thank you.

Barrett runs shirtless through the snow flurries. His chest is scarlet; his breath explodes in steam-puffs. He's slept for a few agitated hours. Now he's going for his morning run. He finds that he's comforted by this utterly usual act, sprinting along Knickerbocker, leaving behind a small, quickly evaporating trail of his own exhalations, like a locomotive rumbling through some still-slumbering, snow-decked town, though Bushwick feels like an actual town, subject to a town's structural logic (as opposed to its true condition of random buildings and rubble-strewn vacant lots, possessed of neither center nor outskirts), only at daybreak, only in its gelid hush, which is soon to end. Soon the delis and shops will open on Flushing, car horns will bleat, the deranged man—filthy and oracular, glowing with insanity like some of the more livid and mortified saints—will take up his station, with a sentry's diligence, on the corner of Knickerbocker and Rock. But at the moment, for the moment, it's actually quiet. Knickerbocker is muffled and nascent and dreamless, empty except for a few cars crawling cautiously along, cutting their headlights into the falling snow.

It's been coming down since midnight. Snow eddies and tumbles as the point of equinox passes, and the sky starts all but imperceptibly turning from its nocturnal blackish brown to the lucid velvety gray of first morning, New York's only innocent sky.

Last night the sky awakened, opened an eye, and saw neither more nor less than Barrett Meeks, homeward bound in a Cossack-style overcoat, standing on the icy platter of Central Park. The sky regarded him, noted him, closed its eye again, and returned to what were, as Barrett can only imagine, more revelatory, incandescent, galaxy-wheeling dreams.

A fear: last night was nothing, a blip, an accidental glimpse behind a celestial curtain, just one of those things. Barrett was no more "chosen" than an upstairs maid would be destined to marry into the family because she happened to see the eldest son naked, on his way to his bath, when he'd assumed the hall to be empty.

Another fear: last night was something, but it's impossible to know, or even guess at, what. Barrett, a perverse, wrong-headed Catholic even in his grade school days (the gray-veined marble Christ at the entrance to the Transfiguration School was *hot*, he had a six-pack and biceps and that mournful, maidenly face), can't remember being told, not even by the most despairing of the nuns, of a vision delivered so arbitrarily, so absent of context. Visions are answers. Answers imply questions.

It's not as if Barrett lacks questions. Who does? But nothing much that begs response from prophet or oracle. Even if the chance were offered, would he want a disciple to run sock-footed down a dim and flickering corridor to interrupt the seer for the purpose of asking, Why do Barrett Meeks's boyfriends all turn out to be sadistic dweebs? Or, What occupation will finally hold Barrett's interest for longer than six months?

What, then—if intention was expressed last night, if that celestial eye opened specifically for Barrett—was the annunciation? What exactly did the light want him to go forth and *do*?

When he got home, he asked Tyler if he'd seen it (Beth was in bed, held in orbit by the increasing gravitational pull of her twilight zone). When Tyler said, "Seen what?" Barrett found, to his surprise, that he was reluctant to say anything about the light. There was of course the obvious explanation—who wants his older brother to suspect he's delusional?—but there was as well a more peculiar sense, for Barrett, of a need for discretion, as if he'd been silently instructed to tell no one. So he made up something quick, about a hit-and-run on the corner of Thames Street.

And then he checked the news.

Nothing. The election, of course. And the fact that Arafat is dying; that the torture at Guantánamo has been confirmed; that a much-anticipated space capsule containing samples taken from the sun has crashed, because its parachute failed to open.

But no lantern-jawed newscaster locked eyes with the camera and said, *This evening the eye of God looked down upon the earth . . .*

Barrett made dinner (Tyler can't be counted on these days to remember that people need to eat periodically, and Beth is too ill). He allowed himself to return to wondering about this last, lost love. Maybe it was that late-night phone conversation, when Barrett knew he was going on too long about the deranged customer who'd insisted that, before he bought a particular jacket, he'd need proof that it had been made under cruelty-free conditions—Barrett can be a bore sometimes, right?—or maybe it was the night he hit the cue ball right off the table, and the lesbian made that remark to her girlfriend (he can be an embarrassment sometimes, too).

He could not, however, contemplate his mysterious misdeeds for long. He'd seen something impossible. Something that, apparently, no one else saw.

He made dinner. He tried to continue compiling his list of reasons for having been dumped.

Now, the following morning, he's going for his run. Why wouldn't he?

As he leaps over a frozen puddle at the corner of Knickerbocker and Thames, the streetlights turn themselves off. Now that a very different light has shown itself to him, he finds himself imagining some connection between the leap and the extinguishment, as if he, Barrett, had ordered the streetlights dimmed, by jumping. As if a lone man, out for his regular three miles, could be the instigator of the new day.

There's that difference, between yesterday and today.

Tyler battles an urge to step up onto the bedroom window-sill. He's not thinking of suicide. Fuck no. And, all right, if he were thinking of suicide, this is only the second floor. The best he might do is break a leg, and maybe—maybe—his skull might kiss the pavement with enough force to produce a concussion. But it would be a pathetic gesture—the loser version of that wearily defiant, ineluctably suave decision to say *That's enough*, and waltz offstage. He has no desire to end up lying on the sidewalk, merely sprained and bruised, akimbo, after a leap into a void that can't have been more than twenty feet.

He's not thinking suicide, he's thinking merely of going

into the storm; of being more stingingly assaulted by wind and snow. The trouble (one of the troubles) with this apartment is one can only be inside it, looking out a window, or outside, on the street, looking up at the window. It would be so fine, so brilliant, to be naked in the weather; to be that available to it.

He contents himself, as he must, by leaning out as far as he can, which produces little more than a frosty wind-smack across his face, and snow pelting his hair.

Back from his run, Barrett enters the apartment, its warmth and its smell: the damp-wood sauna steam exhaled by its ancient radiators; the powdery scent of Beth's medicines; the varnish-and-paint undertones that refuse to dissipate, as if something in this old dump can't fully absorb any attempt at improvement; as if the ghost that is the building itself cannot and will not believe that its walls aren't still bare, smoke-stained plaster, its rooms no longer inhabited by long-skirted women sweating over stoves as their factory-worker husbands sit cursing at kitchen tables. These recently enforced home-improvement smells, this mix of paint and doctor's office, can't do much more than float over a deep ur-smell of ham fat and sweat and spunk, of armpit and whiskey and wet dark rot.

The apartment's warmth brings a tingling numbness to Barrett's skin. On his morning runs he joins the cold, inhabits it the way a long-distance swimmer must inhabit water, and only when he's back inside does he understand that he is in fact half frozen. He's not a comet after all, but a man, hopelessly so, and, being human, must be pulled back in—to the apartment, the boat, the space shuttle—before he perishes of the annihilating beauties, the frigid airless silent places, the helixed and spiraled blackness he'd love to claim as his true home.

A light appeared to him. And vanished again, like some unwelcome memory of his churchly childhood. Barrett has, since the age of fifteen, been adamantly secular, as only an ex-Catholic can be. He released himself, decades ago, from folly and prejudice, from the holy blood that arrived in cardboard cartons by way of UPS; from the stodgy, defeated cheerfulness of priests.

He saw a light, though. The light saw him.

What should he do about that?

For now, it's time for his morning bath.

In the hall, on his way to the bathroom, Barrett passes Tyler and Beth's door, which has yawned open during the night, as do all the doors and drawers and cabinets in this slanty apartment. Barrett pauses, doesn't speak. Tyler is leaning out the window, naked, with his back to the open door, getting snowed upon.

Barrett has always been fascinated by his brother's body. He and Tyler are not particularly similar, as brothers go. Barrett is a bigger guy, not fat (not yet) but ursine, crimson of eye and lip; ginger-furred, possessed (he likes to think) of an enchanted sensual slyness, the prince transformed into wolf or lion, all slumbering large-pawed docility, awaiting, with avid yellow eyes, love's first kiss. Tyler is lithe and stringy, tensely muscled. He can look, even in repose, like an aerialist about to jump from a platform. Tyler's is, somehow, a lean but decorative body, a performer's body; for some reason the word "jaunty" comes to mind. Tyler is irreverent in his body. He exudes the minor devilishness of a circus performer.

He and Barrett are rarely recognized as brothers. And yet, some inscrutable genetic intention is apparent in them. Barrett knows it with certainty, though he couldn't explain. They are similar in ways known only to them. They possess a certain feral knowledge of each other, excrescence and scat. They are never mysterious, one to another, even when they're mysterious to everybody else. It's not that they don't argue or challenge; it's just that nothing one of them does or says ever seems to actually baffle the other. They seem to have agreed, long ago, without ever speaking about it, to keep their affinities secret when they're in company; to bicker at dinner parties, to vie for attention, to carelessly insult and dismiss; to act, in public, like ordinary brothers, and keep their chaste, ardent romance to themselves, as if they were a two-member sect, passing as regular citizens, waiting for their moment to act.

Tyler turns from the window. He could swear he felt eyes on the back of his head, and although there's no one there he feels an essence, a dissolved form that the air in the doorway has not yet entirely forgotten.

And then, the sound of water running in the bathtub. Barrett is back from his run.

How is it that Barrett's presence, whenever he returns from anywhere, still feels like an event to Tyler? The prodigal returned, every single time. It is, after all, just Barrett, the little brother, fat kid clutching a *Brady Bunch* lunch box, weeping as the bus pulled away; adolescent clown who somehow escaped the fate that was all but automatically doled out to the freckled and rotund; Barrett who held court in the high school cafeteria, the bard of Harrisburg, PA; Barrett with whom Tyler has done uncountable childhood battles over turf and tattlings, has vied for their mother's fickle and queenly attentions; Barrett whose sheer creatureliness is more familiar than anyone's, even Beth's; Barrett whose capacious and quirky mind sailed him into Yale, and who, since then, has patiently explained to Tyler, and Tyler alone, the irrefutable logic of his various plans: the post-graduation years of driving around the country (he crossed twenty-seven state lines), picking up jobs (fry cook, motel receptionist, apprentice construction worker) because his mind had grown too full as his hands remained unskilled; then the hustling (because he was too much caught up in romance, too determined to be a latter-day Bryon, it was time for a crash course in the baseness and beastliness of love); the entering of the Ph.D. program (*It's been good for me, it has been, to know for myself that going out into the Mad American Night tends to involve sitting in a Burger King in Seattle because it's the only place open after midnight*) and the leaving of same (*Just because I was wrong about life on the road doesn't mean I wasn't right about not wanting to spend my life arguing about the use of the parenthetical in late James*); the failed Internet venture with his computer-geek boyfriend; the still-thriving café in Fort Green that Barrett abandoned along with his subsequent boyfriend, after the guy came at him with a boning knife; et cetera . . .

All of them seemed, at their times, either like good ideas or (Tyler's preference) fabulously strange ideas, the sort of off-kilter illogic that a smattering of inspired citizens follow to greatness.

None of them, however, seems to have led anywhere in particular.

And now Barrett, the family's tortured Candide, Barrett who seemed so clearly destined for vertiginous heights or true disaster, has committed the most prosaic of human acts— he's lost his apartment and, having nothing like the money required to rent a new one, moved in with his older brother. Barrett has done what was least expected of him—he's be- come another of New York's just-barelies, a guy whose mod- est Hobbitty setup on Horatio Street worked fine as long as the building didn't go co-op.

Still. It's Barrett, and Tyler has not ceased marveling at him in some low-grade but ongoing way.

The current Barrett, the one running bathwater down the hall, is the same Barrett who'd seemed for so long to be the magical child, until it began to look as if that boy would have been the third, unborn son. The Meeks of Harrisburg appear to have stopped one son too soon. They produced Tyler, with his fierce concentration and his athletic ease and his singular gift for music (who knew, at the beginning, just *how* gifted you've got to be?), and then Barrett, who arrived with his array of languid capabilities (he can recite more than a hundred poems; he knows enough about Western philoso- phy to do a lecture series, should anyone ask him to; he picked up nearly fluent French after two months in Paris), but with- out the ability to choose, and persist.

Barrett, now, is about to take a bath.

Tyler will wait until he hears the water stop running. Even with Barrett, there are formalities. Tyler can hang around with his brother once he's in the tub, but can't, for some real but inexplicable reason, watch him enter the water.

Tyler pulls the vial back out of the nightstand drawer, draws himself two lines, perches on the edge of the mattress to Hoover them up. There's nothing, really nothing, like the

morning ones (though this morning is the last, it's his farewell morning); the ones that slap you into beauty, that scour
sloth away, that vaporize the vagaries, the residue of dreams;
that blast you out of slumberland, the shadow realm in which
you wonder, and ask yourself why, and think about going
back to sleep, about how lovely and sweet it would be to just
go on sleeping.

The water stops. Barrett must be immersed.

Tyler puts yesterday's boxer shorts back on (black, emblazoned with tiny white skulls), treads down the hall, opens the
bathroom door. The bathroom is in its way the least upsetting room in the apartment, being the only room that has
not been changed and changed and changed over the last
century-plus. The other rooms are haunted by innumer-
able attempts to erase some past or other with paint or fake
wood paneling, with an acoustic ceiling (the apartment's
most horrific aspect: pockmarked, dingily white squares
made of god-knows-what, Tyler thinks of them as blocks of
freeze-dried sorrow), with carpet that covers linoleum that
covers splintery pine-plank floors. Only the bathroom is essentially as it was, dingy white hexagonal tiles and a pedestal
sink and a toilet that actually still dangles a pull-chain flush
from its tank. The bathroom is a chamber of unmolested
oldness, the only place in which to escape the on-the-cheap
improvements wrought by renters who'd hoped to brighten
things up a bit, who'd imagined that the hibiscus-patterned
contact paper affixed to the kitchen counters, or the word
"Suerte" inexpertly carved into the lintel, would help make
them feel more at home, in this apartment and in the larger
world; and who, all of them, have either moved on by now,
or died.

Barrett is in the tub. There's no denying his capacity for a certain comic grandeur; a pride of being he carries with him everywhere; something royal, something that can in all likelihood only be inherited, never constructed or feigned. Barrett doesn't lie in the tub. He sits straight-backed, blank-faced, like a commuter going home on a train.

He asks Tyler, "What are you doing up?"

Tyler takes a cigarette from the pack he keeps in the medicine cabinet. He doesn't smoke anywhere but in the bathroom, for Beth's sake.

"We left the window open last night. Our bedroom is full of snow."

He taps the pack, violently, before extracting a cigarette. He's not entirely sure why people do that (to concentrate the tobacco?), but he likes doing it, he likes that one sure and punishing *whack* as part of the lighting-up ritual.

Barrett says, "Dreams?"

Tyler lights his cigarette. He goes to the window, cracks it open, blows the smokestream out into the air shaft. His exhalation is answered by a tickle of frigid air, seeping in.

"Some windy joy," he answers. "No specifics. Weather as happiness, but gritty, happiness blowing in unwanted, maybe in a town in Latin America. You?"

"A statue with a hard-on," Barrett says. "A skulking dog. I'm afraid that's it."

They pause as if they were scientists, taking notes.

Barrett asks, "Have you listened to the news yet?"

"No. I'm a little bit afraid to."

"He was still ahead in the polls at six."

"He's not going to win," Tyler says. "I mean, *there were no fucking weapons of mass destruction*. Zero. Zip."

Barrett's attention is briefly diverted by a search, among the shampoo bottles, for one that still contains shampoo. Which is just as well. Tyler knows he can get crazy on the subject, monomaniacal; he can be tiresome about his conviction that if others only *saw*, if they only *understood* . . .

There were no weapons of mass destruction. And we bombed them anyway.

And, by the way, he's destroyed the economy. He's squandered something in the neighborhood of a trillion dollars.

It seems impossible to Tyler that that might not matter. It drives him insane. And now that he's no longer looking out onto his private snow kingdom, now that he's coked himself up from that languid, awake-too-early state, he's not only alert as a rabbit, he's also available, once again, to the forces of fretfulness and dread.

He blows another plume out into the inrushing cold, watches his furls of smoke evaporate in the falling snow.

Barrett says, "What I'm really worried about is Kerry's haircut."

Tyler shuts his eyes, wincingly, as he would at the onset of a headache. He does not want to be, will not be, the one who won't tolerate a joke, the uncle who has to be invited at the holidays even though we all know how he's going to carry on about . . . whatever injustice or betrayal or historical malfeasance he wears like a suit of iron, soldered to his body.

"What I'm worried about," Tyler says, "is Ohio."

"I think it'll be all right," Barrett answers. "I have a feeling. Or, well, I have hope."

He has hope. Hope is an old jester's cap by now. Faded motley, with that little tin bell at the tip. Who has the energy to wear it anymore? But who's courageous enough to doff it, leave it crumpled in the lane? Not Tyler.

"I do too," he says. "I have hope and belief and even a particle or two of actual faith."

"How are you doing with Beth's song?"

"I'm a little stuck," Tyler says. "But I think I made some progress last night."

"Good. That's good."

"Giving her a song seems kind of . . . small, don't you think?"

"Of course not. I mean, what kind of wedding gift do you think would mean more to her? A BlackBerry?"

"It's so impossible."

"Writing songs is hard. Well, pretty much everything is hard, right?"

"I guess," Tyler says.

Barrett nods. They pass through a moment of silence as old as either of them can remember, the quietude of growing up together, of sleeping in the same room; the shared quiet that has always been their true element, interrupted of course by talks and fights and farts and laughter over the farts but essential, the atmosphere to which they've always returned, a field of soundless oxygen made up of their combined molecules.

Tyler says, "Mom got struck by lightning on a golf course."

"Uh, you know, I know that."

"Betty Ferguson said at the memorial that she'd been three under par that day."

"I know that, too."

"Big Boy got hit by the same car, twice. Two years in a

row. And it didn't kill him either time. Then he choked to death on a Snickers bar at Halloween."

"Tyler, really."

"Then we got another beagle and named him Big Boy Two, and he got squashed by the son of the woman who'd hit Big Boy One, twice. It was the first time the woman's son had driven by himself, it was his sixteenth birthday."

"Why are you saying all this?"

"I'm just listing the impossibilities that happened anyway," Tyler says.

"So, like, Bush won't be reelected."

Tyler doesn't say, And Beth will live. He doesn't say, The chemo is working.

He says, "I just want this fucking song to be good."

"It will be."

"You sound like Mom."

Barrett says, "I *am* like Mom. And you know, really, it won't matter if the song isn't great. Not to Beth."

"It'll matter to me."

Barrett's sympathy blooms in his eyes, which darken for Tyler the way their father's do. Although their father is not an especially gifted father, this is one of his talents. He has the ability, when needed, to perform this little eye-shift, a deepening and dilating that says to his sons, *You don't have to matter any more than you do right now.*

They should call him, it's been, what, more than a week now. Maybe two.

Why did he marry Marva so soon after Mom died? Why did they move to Atlanta, what do they *do* down there?

Who *is* this guy, where did the plaid come from, how can he love Marva—Marva's okay, she's fun in her crude, shock-the-boys way, you learn not to stare at the scar, but how can their dad cease to be Mom's solicitous penitent? The deal was always so clear. She was the cherished and endangered one (lightning found her), it was right there on her face (the milk-blue Slavic fineness of it, her hand-carved quality, her porcelain glaze). Their father was the designated driver, the guy who enforced naps, the one who got panicky when she was half an hour late; the middle-aged boy who'd sit under her window in the rain until he caught his death.

And now, this person. This man who wears Tommy Bahama shorts, and Tevas. This guy who rockets around Atlanta with Marva in a Chrysler Imperial convertible, blowing cigarillo smoke up at whatever constellations appear over Georgia.

It's probably easier on him, being this guy. Tyler doesn't, won't, begrudge it.

And, really, their father was released from paternal duty years and years ago, wasn't he? It may have occurred as early as those drinking sessions with Barrett, during the days after their mother's service.

They were seventeen and twenty-two. They just hung around the house like stray dogs for a few days, in briefs and socks, drinking down the supply (the scotch and vodka led to the gin, which led to the off-brand tequila, which led eventually to a quarter-full bottle of Tia Maria, and an inch of Drambuie that had probably been there twenty years or more).

They languished for days in the suddenly famous living room, surrounded by all the ordinary things that had so abruptly become *her* things. Tyler and Barrett, sloppy and scared and shocked, getting hammered in their briefs and socks; it was (maybe it was) the night they turned a particular corner . . .

Do you ever think?

What?

They were lying together on the sofa that had always been there, the crappy beat-up biscuit-colored sofa that was managing, as best it could, its promotion from threadbare junk to holy artifact.

You know.

What if I don't know?

You fucking do.

Okay, yeah. Yes. I, too, wonder if Dad worried so much about every single little goddamned thing . . .

That he summoned it.

Thanks. I couldn't say it.

That some god or goddess heard him, one time too many, getting panicky about whether she'd been carjacked at the mall, or had, like, hair cancer . . .

That they delivered the thing even he couldn't imagine worrying about.

It's not true.

I know.

But we're both thinking about it.

That may have been their betrothal. That may have been when they took their vows: We are no longer siblings, we are mates, starship survivors, a two-man crew wandering the crags and crevices of a planet that may not be inhabited by anyone but us. We no longer need, or want, a father.

Still, they really have to call him. It's been way too long.

"I know," Barrett says. "I know it'll matter to you. But I

think you should remember that it won't, to her. Not in the same way."

Barrett, bluff-chested, naked in graying water, is in particular possession of his pink-white, grandly mortified glow.

"I'm going to make some coffee," Tyler says.

Barrett stands up in the tub, streaming bathwater, a hybrid of stocky robust manliness and plump little boy.

This peculiarity: Tyler is untroubled by the sight of Barrett emerging from his bathwater. It is, for mysterious reasons, only Barrett's immersion that's difficult for Tyler to witness.

Might that have to do with endangerment, and rescue? Duh.

Another peculiarity: Knowledge of one's deeper motives, the sources of one's peccadilloes and paranoias, doesn't necessarily make much difference.

"I'm going to go to the shop," Barrett says.

"Now?"

"I feel like being alone there."

"It's not like you don't have your own room. I mean, am I crowding you?"

"Shut up. Okay?"

Tyler tosses Barrett a towel from the rack.

"It seems right, that the song is about snow," Barrett says.

"It seemed right when I started it."

"I know. I mean, it all seems right when you start it, it seems infinitely promising and inspired and great . . . I'm not trying to be *profound*, or anything."

Tyler lingers for a final moment, to fully feel the charge. They do the eye thing, once more, for each other. It's simple, it's undramatic, there's nothing moist or abashed, nothing actually ardent, going on, but they pass something back and

forth. Call it recognition, though it's more than that. It's recognition, and it's the mutual conjuring of their ghost brother,
the third one who didn't quite manage to be born, and
so, being spectral—less than spectral, being *never*—is their
medium, their twinship, their daemon; the boy (he'll never
grow past the pink-faced, holy gravitas of the cherubim)
who is the two of them, combined.

———

B arrett dries off. The bathwater, now that he's out of the tub, has turned from its initial, steaming clarity to a tepid murk, as it always does. Why does that happen? Is it soap residue, or Barrett residue—the sloughed-off outermost layer of city grime and deceased epidermis and (he can't help thinking this) some measure of his essence, his little greeds and vanities, his self-admiration, his habit of sorrow, washed away, for now, with soap, left behind, to spiral down the drain.

He stares for a moment longer at his bathwater. It's the usual water. It's no different the morning after the night he's seen something he can't really have seen.

Why, exactly, would Tyler believe this was a good morning to return them to the story of their mother?

A time-snap: Their mother reclines on the sofa (which is here now, right here in their Bushwick living room), smoking, cheerfully bleary on a few old-fashioneds (Barrett likes her best when she drinks—it emphasizes her aspect of extravagant and knowing defeat; the wry, amused carelessness she lacks when sober, when she's forced by too much clarity to remember that a life of regal disappointment, while painful, is also Chekhovian; grave, and rather grand). Barrett is nine. His mother looks at him with drink-sparked eyes, smiles knowingly, as if she's got a pet leopard lying at her feet, and says, "You're going to have to watch out for your older brother, you know."

Barrett waits, mutely, sitting on the sofa's edge, at the curve of his mother's knees, for meaning to arrive. His mother takes a drag, a sip, a drag.

"Because, sweetheart," she says, "let's face it. Let's be candid, can we be candid?"

Barrett acknowledges that they can. Wouldn't anything other than total candor between a mother and her nine-year-old son be an aberration?

She says, "Your brother is a lovely boy. A lovely, lovely boy."

"Uh-huh."

"And you" (drag, sip) "are something else."

Barrett blinks, damp-eyed with incipient dread. He is about to be told that he's subservient to Tyler; that he's the portly little quipster, the comic relief, while his older brother can slay a boar with a single arrow, split a tree with one caress of an axe.

She says, "Some magic has been granted to you. I'm damned if I know where it came from. But I knew it. I knew it right away. When you were born."

Barrett keeps blinking back the tears he's determined not to shed in front of her, though he wonders, with increasing urgency, what, exactly, she's talking about.

"Tyler is popular," she says. "Tyler is good-looking. Tyler can throw a football . . . well, he can throw it pretty far, and in the direction footballs are supposed to go."

"I know," Barrett says.

What strange impatience rises now to his mother's face? Why does she look at him as if he were sycophantically eager, desperate to please some doddering aunt by pretending surprise over every twist in a story he's known by heart, for years?

"Those whom the gods would destroy . . ." his mother says, blowing smoke up into the crystals of the modest dome-shaped chandelier that clings like an upside-down tiara to the living room ceiling. Barrett isn't sure whether she can't, or won't, finish the line.

"Tyler is a good guy," Barrett says, for no reason he can name, beyond the fact that it seems he has to say something.

His mother speaks upward, toward the chandelier. She says, "My point exactly."

This will all start making sense. It will, soon. The square crystals of the chandelier, worried by the electric fan, each crystal the size of a sugar cube, put out their modest, prismed spasms of light.

His mother says, "You may need to help him out, a little. Later. Not now. He's fine, now. He's cock o' the walk."

Cock o' the walk. A virtue?

She says, "I just want you to, well . . . remember this conversation we're having. Years from now. Remember that your brother may need help from you. He may need a kind of help you can't possibly imagine, at the age of ten."

"I'm nine," Barrett reminds her.

Almost thirty years later, having arrived at the future to which his mother was referring, Barrett pulls the plug on the bathtub. There's the familiar sound of water being sucked away. It's a morning like any other, except . . .

The vision is the first event of any consequence, in how many years, about which Barrett hasn't told Tyler; which he continues not mentioning to Tyler. Barrett has never, since he was a kid, been alone with a secret.

He has, of course, never kept a secret quite like this.

He'll tell Tyler, he will, but not now, not yet. Barrett isn't ready for Tyler's skepticism, or his valiant efforts at be-lief. He's really and truly not ready for Tyler to be worried about him. He can't bring himself to be another cause for concern, not with Beth getting neither better nor worse.

A terrible thing: Barrett finds sometimes that he wants Beth either to recover or die.

The endless waiting, the uncertainty (higher white-cell count last week, that's good, but the tumors on her liver are neither growing nor shrinking, that's not so good), may be worse than grieving.

A surprise: There's no one driving the bus. There are five different doctors now, none of them actually in charge, and sometimes their stories don't match up. They make ef-forts, they're not bad doctors (except for Scary Steve, the chemo guy), they're not negligent, they try this and they try that, but Barrett (and Tyler, and probably Beth, though she's never talked about it) had imagined a warrior, someone kind and august, someone who'd be *sure*. Barrett had not expected this disorganized squadron—all upsettingly young, except for Big Betty—who know the language of healing, who reel off seven-syllable terms (tending to forget, or to disregard, the fact that the words are incomprehensible to anyone who isn't a doctor), who can operate the machinery, but who, purely and simply, don't know what's going to work, or what's going to happen.

Barrett can keep this one about the celestial light private, for a while. It's not an announcement Tyler needs to receive.

Barrett has, naturally enough, Googled every possible malady (torn retina, brain tumor, epilepsy, psychotic break) that's presaged by a vision of light. Nothing quite fits.

Although he's seen something extraordinary, and hopes it isn't the precursor of a mortal ailment he failed to find on the Internet, he has not been instructed, he has not been transformed, there's been no message or command, he is exactly who he was last night.

However. The question arises: Who was he last night? Has he in fact been altered in some subtle way, or has he simply been rendered more conscious of the particulars of his own ongoing condition? It's a hard one to answer.

An answer might account for how and why Barrett and Tyler have lived so randomly (they, the National Merit boys— well, Barrett; Tyler was a runner-up—club presidents, Tyler crowned king of the fucking prom); why they happened to meet Liz when he and Tyler went, as each other's date, to what has lived on as the Worst Party in History; why the three of them escaped the party and passed midnight together in some divey Irish pub; why Liz would eventually introduce Beth, newly arrived from Chicago; Beth who in no way resembles any of Tyler's previous girlfriends, and with whom he'd fallen so immediately in love that he resembled some captive animal, fed for years on what its keepers believed to be its natural diet and then suddenly, one day, by accident, given what it actually ate, in the wild.

None of it has ever felt predetermined. It's sequential, but not exactly orderly. It's all been going to this party instead of that one, happening to meet someone who knew someone who by the evening's end had fucked you in a doorway on Tenth Avenue or given you K for the first time or said something shockingly kind, out of nowhere, and then gone away forever, promising to call; or, with an equally haphazard aspect, happening to meet someone who'll change everything, forever.

And now it's a Tuesday in November. Barrett has gone for his morning run, had his morning bath. He's going to work. What is there to do but what he always does? He'll sell the wares (it'll be slow today, because of the weather). He'll continue with his exercise regimen and the no-carbs diet that will not make any difference to Andrew but will, might, help Barrett feel more agile and tragic, less like a badger besotted by a lion cub.

Will he see the light again? What if he doesn't? Maybe he'll grow old as a tale-teller who once saw something inexplicable; a UFO person, a Bigfoot person, a codger who experienced a brief, wondrous sighting of something inexplicable, and then went on about the business of getting older; who is part of the ongoing subhistory of crackpots and delusionals, the legions of geezers who know what they saw, decades ago, and if you don't believe it, young one, that's all right, maybe one day you, too, will see something you can't explain, and then, well, then I guess you'll know.

Beth is looking for something.

The trouble: She can't seem to remember what it is.

She knows this much: She's been careless, she's misplaced . . . what? Something that matters, something that must be found, because . . . it's needed. Because she'll be held accountable when its absence is noticed.

She's searching a house, although she's not sure if it (what?) is here. It seems possible. Because she's been in this house before. She recognizes it, or remembers it, in the way she remembers the houses of her childhood. The house multiplies into the houses in which she lived, variously, until she went away to college. There's the gray-and-white-striped wallpaper of the house in Evanston, the French doors from Winnetka (were they really this narrow?), the crown molding from the second house in Winnetka (was it wound in these white plaster leaves, was there this suggestion of wise but astonished eyes, peering through the leaves?).

They'll be back soon. Somebody will be back soon. Someone stern. The harder Beth searches, though, the less sense she has of what it is she's lost. It's small, isn't it? Spherical? Is it too small to be visible? It might be. But that doesn't alter the urgency of its discovery.

She's the girl in the fairy tale, told to turn snow into gold by morning.

She can't do that, of course she can't, but there seems to be snow everywhere, it's falling from the ceiling, snowdrifts shimmer in the corners. She remembers dreaming about searching through a house, when what she needs to do is turn snow into gold, how could she have forgotten . . .

She looks down at her feet. Although the floor is dusted with snow, she can see that she's standing on a door, a trapdoor, contiguous with the floorboards, made apparent only by its pair of brass hinges and its tiny brass knob, no bigger than a gumball.

Her mother gives her a penny for a gumball machine outside the A&P. She doesn't know how to tell her mother that one of the gumballs is poisoned, no one should put a penny into this machine, but her mother is so delighted by Beth's delight, she's got to put the penny in, hasn't she?

There's a trapdoor at her feet, in the sidewalk in front of the A&P. It's snowing here, too.

Her mother urges her to put the penny into the slot. Beth can hear laughter, coming from underneath the door.

An annihilating force, a swirling orb of malevolence, is what's laughing under the trapdoor. Beth knows this to be true. Is the door beginning, ever so slowly, to open?

She's holding the penny. Her mother says, "Put it in." It comes to her that the penny is what she thought she was searching for. She seems to have found it, by accident.

Tyler sits in the kitchen, sipping coffee and doing one last line. He's still wearing the boxer shorts, and has put on Barrett's old Yale sweatshirt, its grimacing bulldog faded, by now, from red to a faint, candyish pink. Tyler sits at the table Beth found on the street, cloudy gray Formica that's chipped away in one corner, a ragged-edged gap the shape of the state of Idaho. When this table was new, people expected domed cities to rise on the ocean floor. They believed that they lived on the brink of a holy and ecstatic conjuring of metal and glass and silent, rubberized speed.

The world is older now. It can, at times, seem very old indeed.

They will not reelect George Bush. They cannot re-elect George Bush.

Tyler pushes the thought out of his mind. It would be foolish to spend this lambent early hour obsessing. He's got a song to finish.

So as not to awaken Beth, he leaves his guitar in the corner. He whisper-sings, a cappella, the verse he wrote last night.

To walk the frozen halls at night
To find you on your throne of ice
To melt this sliver in my heart
Oh, that's not what I came for
No, that's not what I came for.

Hmm. It's crap, is it?

The trouble is . . .

The trouble is he's determined to write a wedding song that won't be all treacle and devotion, but won't be cool or calm, either. How, exactly, do you write a song for a dying bride? How do you account for love and mortality (the real thing, not some till-death-do-us-part throwaway) without morbidity?

It needs to be a serious song. Or, rather, it needs not to be a frivolous song.

The melody will help. Please, let the melody help. This time, though, the lyrics need to come first. Once the lyrics feel right (once they feel less wrong), he'll lay them over . . . a minimal tune, something simple and direct, not childish of course but possessed of a childlike, beginner's earnestness, a beginner's innocence of tricks. It should be all major chords, with one minor, at the end of the bridge—that single jolt of gravitas; that moment when the lyrics' romantic solemnity departs from the contrast of its upbeat chords and matches—fleetingly—a darkness in the music itself. The song should reside in the general vicinity of Dylan, of the Velvet Underground. It should not be faux-Dylan, not fake Lou Reed; it should be original (*original*, naturally; preferably *unprecedented*; preferably *tinged with genius*), but it helps, it helps a little, to aim in a general direction. Dylan's righteous banishment of sentimentality, Reed's ability to mingle passion with irony.

The melody should have . . . a shimmering honesty, it should be egoless, no *Hey, I can really play this guitar, do you get that?* Because the song is an unvarnished love-shout, an implorement tinged with . . . anger? Something like anger, but the anger of a philosopher, the anger of a poet, an anger directed at the transience of the world, at its heartbreaking beauty that collides constantly with our awareness of the fact that everything gets taken away; that we're being shown marvels but reminded, always, that they don't belong to us, they're sultan's treasures, we're lucky (we're expected to feel lucky) to have been invited to see them at all.

And there's this, as well. The song has to be infused with . . . if not anything as banal as hope, an assertion of an ardency that can, if this is humanly possible (and the song must insist that it is), follow the bride in her journey to the netherworld, abide there with her. It has to be a song in which a husband and singer declares himself to be not only a woman's life-mate, but her death-mate as well, although he, helpless, unconsulted, will keep on living.

Good luck with that one.

He pours himself more coffee, draws out a final, really

final, line on the tabletop. Maybe he's just not . . . *awake* enough to be gifted. Maybe one day, why not today, he'll bust out of his lifelong drowse.

Would "shiver" be better than "sliver"? *To melt this shiver in my heart?*

No. It wouldn't.

That repetition at the end—is it forceful or cheap?

Should he try for a half-rhyme with "heart"? Is it too sentimental to use the word "heart" at all?

He needs a looser association. He needs something that implies a man who wants the ice shard to remain in his chest, who's learned to love the sensation of being pierced.

To walk the frozen halls at night
To find you on your throne of ice

Maybe it's not as bad as it sounds this early in the morning. That's a possibility.

But still. If Tyler were the real thing, if he were meant to do this, wouldn't he have more confidence? Wouldn't he feel . . . *guided,* somehow?

Never mind that he's forty-three, and still playing in a bar.

He will not come to his senses. That's the siren song of advancing age. He can't, he won't, deny the snag in his heart (there's that *word* again). He can feel it, an undercurrent in his bloodstream, this urge that's utterly his own. No one ever said to him, why don't you use your degree in political science to write songs, why don't you blow the modest inheritance your mother left by sitting in ever-smaller rooms, strumming a guitar. It's his open secret, the self inside the self, secret because he believes he knows within himself a brilliance, or at least a penetrating clarity, that hasn't come out yet. He's still producing approximations, and it vexes him that most people (not Beth, not Barrett, just everybody else) see him as a sad case, a middle-aged bar singer (no, make that a middle-aged bar*tender*, who's permitted by the owner to sing on Friday and Saturday nights), when he knows (he knows) that he's still nascent, no prodigy of course, but the music and poetry move slowly in him, great songs hover over his head, and there are moments, real moments, when he feels so certain he can reach them, he can almost literally pull them out of the air, and he tries, lord how he tries, but what he grabs hold of is never quite it.

Fail. Try again. Fail better. Right?

He sings the first two lines again, softly, to himself. He hopes they'll open into . . . something. Something magical, and obscurely on target, and . . . *good.*

> *To walk the frozen halls at night*
> *To find you on your throne of ice*

He sings quietly in the kitchen, with its faint gassy smell and its pale blue walls (they must, once, have been aquamarine), its tacked-up photographs of Burroughs and Bowie and Dylan, and (Beth's) Faulkner and Flannery O'Connor. If he can write a beautiful song for Beth, if he can sing it to her at their wedding and know that it's a proper testament— a true gift, not just another near miss, another nice try, but a song that lands, that lances, that's gentle but faceted, gleaming, gem-hard . . .

Give it one more go, then.

He starts singing again, as Beth dreams in the next room. He sings quietly to his lover, his bride to be, his dying girl, the girl for whom this song and, probably, really, all the songs are meant. He sings into the brightening air of the room.

Barrett has gotten dressed. The tight (too tight? fuck it—if you present yourself as a beauty, people tend to believe you) wool pants, the Clash T-shirt (worn down to pearl-gray translucence), the ostentatiously ragged sweater that drapes limp and indolent almost to his knees.

Here he is, bathed, hair-gelled, dressed for the day. Here's his reflection in his bedroom mirror, here's the room in which he currently resides: Shinto-inspired, just a mattress and a low table, the walls and floor painted white, Barrett's private sanctuary from the funky-junk museum that is the rest of Tyler and Beth's apartment.

He takes out his cell phone. Liz's phone will be turned

off, of course, but he should tell her he's going to open the shop this morning.

"Hey, it's Liz, leave a message."

He's still surprised, sometimes, by the clipped force of her voice, when it transmits unaccompanied by her animated, rather off-kilter face (she's one of those women who insists, successfully, on her own beauty—Barrett has learned from her; on the assertion that a hooked jut of nose and a wide, thin-lipped mouth is, must be, added to the list of desirable features), the careless gray tangle of her hair.

Barrett speaks into (onto?) her voice mail.

"Hi. I'm going in early, just to lurk around, so if you and Andrew want to stay snuggled up, go ahead. I'll open. And it's not like there's going to be any customers on a day like this. Bye."

Andrew. The most ideal being among Barrett's inner population; graceful and inscrutable as a figure from the Parthenon friezes; Barrett's singular experience of the godly. Andrew is as close as Barrett has come to a sense of divine presence in the world.

A minor epiphany circles his head like a persistent fly. Did his most recent boyfriend leave so casually because he sensed Barrett's fixation on Andrew, which Barrett never, ever, mentioned? Is it possible that the departed boy perceived himself as an imitation, of sorts; as the most possessable version of Andrew's offhand, no-big-deal beauty; Andrew who will do, for now and possibly forever, as the most persuasive living evidence of God's genius, coupled with God's inscrutable propensity for sculpting some of the clay with a degree of attention to the symmetries and precisions He (She?) withholds from most of the population at large?

No. Probably not. The guy wasn't, frankly, a particularly subtle or intuitive thinker, and Barrett's devotion to Andrew carries no hint of actual possibility. Barrett adores Andrew the way one might a Phidias Apollo. You don't expect a marble sculpture to step down off its museum pedestal and take you in its arms. No one dumps a lover because the lover is besotted by art. Right?

Who doesn't want—who doesn't need—a moon at which to marvel, a fabled city of glass and gold on the far side of the ocean? Who would insist that his corporeal lover— the guy in his bed, the man who forgets to throw his used Kleenexes away, who used the last of the coffee before he left for work—be the moon or the city?

If Barrett's latest ex did in fact desert him because Barrett maintains a private fascination with a boy he'll never have . . . That might, in some perverse way, be good to know. Barrett prefers a version in which the vanished lover turns out to have been unreasonable, or paranoid, or even a little bit insane.

On his way out, Barrett pauses, again, at the open door of Tyler and Beth's bedroom. Beth is asleep. Tyler must be in the kitchen, cranking on coffee. Barrett is glad, of course— everybody is—that Tyler has stopped doing drugs.

Barrett stands for a moment in the bedroom doorway, watching Beth sleep. She's as frail and ivory-colored as a co-matose princess, slumbering through decades, waiting for the spell to be broken. She looks, strangely enough, less sick when she sleeps; when her conversation and her concerns and her mannerisms aren't so clearly struggling to survive the failing of her body.

Has Barrett been given a sign about Beth? Does the fact

that some immense inhuman intelligence elected to appear to him at this particular time have anything to do with Beth slipping off into more and more sleep?

Or was the vision just a little flesh-stone pressing against his cerebral cortex? How will he feel when, a year or so from now, someone in an emergency room tells him they could have caught that tumor if only he'd acted sooner?

He's not going to see a doctor. If he had a regular doctor (he imagines her as Swedish, sixty-plus, stern but not fanatical about his health; prone to mild, mock-serious scoldings about his modest amalgam of less-than-salubrious pleasures), he'd call her. Given that he's uninsured, subject to clinics and the ministrations of medical students who are learning on the job, he can't seem to bring himself to face the questions an unknown doctor would pose about his history of mental health. It's only possible for him to imagine discussing the celestial light with someone who knows him, already, as fundamentally sane.

Would he rather risk death than embarrassment? It seems that he would.

Quietly (he's still in his socks, shoes are left by the front door, a strange local custom, given the apartment's less-than-tidy nature), Barrett walks into the room and stands beside the bed, listening to the steady murmur of Beth's breathing.

He can smell her—the lavender soap they all use, mingled with a smell he can only think of as *womanly*, a ripe cleanliness that's somehow enhanced and deepened by sleep, all mixed up now with the powder and nettle of her medicines, the strangest roil of pharmaceutical immaculacy and some sour chamomile-family herb that has in all likelihood been gathered for centuries in bogs and marshes, along with a sickroom smell he can only think of as electric, the inde-scribable cauterizing invisible whatever that runs through wires hidden in the walls of rooms in which someone is mortally ill.

He bends over, looks closely at Beth's face, which is pretty, pretty enough, but, at the same time, better than pretty, more personal. If prettiness implies a certain quality of banal resemblance, Beth looks like no one but herself. Her lips, slightly parted, issuing the faint whistle of her breath, are puffy and puckery; her nose some remnant of an Asian an-cestor, with its flattened humility, its little slits of nostrils; her eyelids blue-white, the lashes sable; the pallid pinkish melon scalp of her chemo-induced baldness.

She's lovely, but she's not a great beauty, and her accom-plishments are charming, but minor. She's a good baker. She has fashion sense. She's smart, an avid reader. She's kind to just about everyone.

Is it possible that the light, by choosing to appear to him as Beth fades, meant something about a life that continues beyond the limits of the flesh?

Or is that some messianic bent of Barrett's?

Could that be why his lover left? Because he's too prone to Signs of Significance?

Barrett bends low, puts his face so close to Beth's that he can feel her breath on his chin. She's alive. She's alive right now. Her eyelids twitch over a dream.

He imagines her dreams as pale and buoyant, bright even in extremis; no lurking invisible terrors, no shriek of anni-hilation, no innocent-seeming heads turning to reveal black holes instead of eyes, or teeth like razors. He hopes that's true.

A moment later he stands, abruptly, as if somebody had called his name. He almost stumbles backward over the fact that Beth is being taken out so early, and that her absence will be felt by a small body of people, but will otherwise go unnoticed. It's not a surprise. But it strikes him now with particular force. Is it more tragic, or is it less, to slip so quietly and briefly into and out of the world? To have added, and altered, so little.

An unwelcome thought: Beth's primary accomplishment may be to have loved and been loved by Tyler. Tyler, who sees something invisible even to everyone else who loves her. She is widely loved. But Tyler adores her, Tyler is fascinated by her, Tyler finds her extraordinary.

As does Barrett, though he does so because Tyler does. Still. Beth will have been loved ardently by a main man and a backup man. She will have been, in a certain sense, doubly married.

How exactly will Tyler live on after she's departed? Barrett adores Beth, and (as far as he knows) she adores him in return, but it's Tyler, and Tyler alone, who delivers the daily ministrations. How will he live not only with the loss of her but also the loss of the purpose she's created, these past two years? Caring for Beth has been his career. He's played and composed his music on the side, whenever he's not too urgently needed.

Somehow, Barrett has failed to fully apprehend it until now: Tyler is worried, Tyler is aggrieved, but also, since Beth's diagnosis, he's been more content than Barrett has seen him in years. Tyler would never admit it, not even to himself, but seeing to Beth—comforting her, feeding her, keeping track of her medication, arguing with her doctors—has made him successful. Here is something he can do, and can do well, as the music flicks teasingly around him, just out of reach. And there is, probably, isn't there, something dreadful but calming about the certainty of failure, in the end. Hardly anyone becomes a great musician. No one can reach into the body of a loved one, and scrape the cancer away. One blames oneself for the former. One has nothing to say about the latter.

Barrett places his hand, gently, onto Beth's forehead, though he hadn't exactly intended to. He feels as if he's watching his hand perform an act he didn't ask of it. Beth murmurs, but doesn't awaken.

Barrett does his best to transmit some kind of healing force, through the palm of his hand. Then he walks back out of the sickroom, returns to the comforting normalcy of the hall, and heads for the kitchen, where Tyler is awake, where coffee has been made, where the rampancy of life, even in its most rudimentary form, plays like an enchanted piper; where Tyler, suitor and swain, ferocious of brow, thin but athletically tendoned legs protruding from boxer shorts, does what he can to prepare for his forthcoming marriage.

T he marriage thing is very weird," Liz says to Andrew. They're standing on her roof, with snow billowing around them. They've come up to the roof for the shock of it, after a night that just rolled off the time-spool (my god, Andrew, it's four in the morning; shit, Andrew, how'd it suddenly get to be five *thirty*, we've got to get some *sleep*). They've been too high to have sex, but there were moments, there were moments, during the night, when it seemed to Liz that she was explaining herself entirely; that she was able to hold her very being in her outstretched palms and say, here I am, here's the golden box all tricked open, every hidden drawer and false bottom released; here is my honor and my generosity, here are my wounds and my fears, the real as well as the imaginary; here is what I see and think and feel; here is my acuity and my hope and my way of turning a phrase; here is the . . . *me*-ness of me, the tangible but inchoate entity that shifts and buzzes within the flesh, the central part that simply *is*, the part that finds it wonderful and appalling and strange to be a woman named Liz who lives in Brooklyn and owns a shop; the unnamed and unnameable; that which God would recognize after the flesh has fallen away.

Really, who needed to have sex?

Now she is quieting, returning, reconnecting (with both sorrow and gratitude) to her more corporeal self, the self that still blazes with its own light and heat but is tethered by all the sinewy little strings—the self that's capable of pettiness and irritation, skepticism and needless anxiety. She is no longer aloft, no longer spreading a star-studded cloak over the nocturnal woods; she is still full of mingled magic but she is also a woman standing on a roof with her much-younger boyfriend, pelted by blowing snow, a denizen of the ordinary world, someone who might say, *The marriage thing is very weird.*

"I don't know," Andrew says. "Do you really think so?"

He is uncannily lovely in the snowblown dawn, luminously pale as a Giotto saint, snowflakes caught in his cropped red hair. Liz passes through a queasy little thrill of astonishment—this boy is interested in her. They'll both move on, she knows that, they have no choice, given the fact that he's twenty-eight (imagine being twenty-eight!). Fifty-two-year-old Liz Compton will figure in his still-forming life for as long as she does. She doesn't mind, she doesn't really mind, and besides, he's here now, glassy-eyed from the night, wrapped in one of her blankets, porcelain in the early light, hers until he isn't anymore.

She says, "Oh, well, I *get* it, but I don't think they'd be getting married if she wasn't . . . if she were well. I guess, really, I wonder if it might be embarrassing for her. Like taking a sick child to Disney World."

Too cynical, Liz. Too harsh. Stay with the night world, speak to this boy in the language of earnest kindness that he speaks, himself.

He says, "Um, I know what you mean. But I think, you know, if I was really sick, I wouldn't mind. If, like, somebody wanted to declare his love like that."

"I suppose I wonder how much Tyler is doing this for Beth and how much he's doing it for himself."

Andrew looks at her uncomprehendingly. His drugged-out eyes are bright but depthless.

Is she talking too much? Is it possible that in their night-long orgy of conversation, she's been boring him? Was the bestowed treasure really just a woman of a certain age, going on and on and on?

The bonds of the flesh are back. Here again are the doubts and the little self-mutilations, nasty but oddly comforting as well, so familiar are they.

"Maybe," he says. "I mean, I don't know them all that well."

He is shutting down. She's exhausted him. Still, she's not quite ready to let it go—the ragged ends of the glorious night, the conviction that everything can be understood.

"Let's go back inside," she says. She's losing something precious, up here in the snowy dawn. It's almost as if the wind is blowing her expansiveness away and leaving only the pebbles of her skepticism, her little rosary of complaints.

"No, wait a minute," Andrew says. "I think . . ."

She waits. He's working something out. He stands snow-sparked, berobed, deciding what it is he thinks.

He says, "I think people worry too much. I think we should go ahead and make mistakes. Like, we should get married. We should have babies. Even if, you know, our reasons may not be all that noble and pure. I think maybe you could be noble and pure all your life and end up, well, pretty much alone."

"Maybe," she answers. "That might very well be true."

"Shit gets messy. It should get messy."

"Up to a point," she says. "Hey, are you shivering?"

"Um, a little."

"Let's go back down, then," she says.

She kisses his cold lips.

In the kitchen, Barrett pours himself a half-cup of coffee, his morning allowance. Tyler, gone to Tyler world, hums a song and beats time, softly, with a fingertip on the table.

It's rare for Barrett to wonder what to say to Tyler. Barrett holds his coffee mug, as if that were his singular purpose. Inevitably, it takes Tyler a moment to return from his parallel dimension. In the kitchen, in the mornings, Barrett always speaks first.

Tyler says, "Do you really want to go to the shop three hours before it opens?"

Tyler can speak normally, normally enough, but he isn't quite back from the realm. Although he's stopped humming, the music still blares in his head. Barrett suspects Tyler must feel, at times, especially in the mornings, when he's most fervent and hopeful about his music, that conducting an ordinary conversation is like shouting to be heard on a construction site.

Barrett doesn't answer. He'd like to answer. He expects to answer. At the moment, however, he's struggling to remember what he says in these kitchen conversations—these daily, brotherly launchings into the day ahead (safe travels, pilgrim)—and how, exactly, he says it.

He has a secret, now. He's keeping something from Tyler.

A surprise: It throws him off.

A subsequent surprise: There is, it seems, an act, a quality of impersonation, involved in being Barrett.

Tyler says, "Hello?"

Which is funny. They have, for the first time in Barrett's memory, reversed positions. Barrett has, since childhood, been the one who reels Tyler back in from his finger-tapping contemplations.

Barrett snaps to.

"I do," he says. "It'll be nice, being alone in there. It'll be good for reading."

He sounds very much like himself, doesn't he? He hopes he does. At least, Tyler doesn't seem to be looking at him strangely.

"You can read here. You can be alone here."

"Now *you* sound like Mom."

"We're both like Mom," Tyler says.

"Do you think that means we can't get struck by lightning?"

"Explain."

"It's like, a woman gets struck by lightning on a golf course and then, years later, one of her sons gets struck by lightning too. How plausible is that?"

"The odds are exactly the same."

"I sometimes wonder how you live with such a modest sense of romance," Barrett says.

"Superstition and romance are not the same thing."

"But don't you ever wonder where Mom is?"

Tyler looks at him as if he's made a rude and tasteless remark. "Of course I do."

"Do you think she's just . . . gone?"

"I don't like to think that."

A droplet, long accumulating, falls from the rim of the faucet into a soaking saucepan, makes a tiny *ping*. The fluorescent ring on the ceiling, covered by Beth with a red silk scarf which filters and pinkens the light, emits its low buzz.

"Do you ever wonder if the Catholics are right?" Barrett asks.

"They're not. Next question."

"Somebody's got to be right. Why not the Catholics?"

"You're sounding a little crazy."

The rim of the kitchen table, ridged aluminum, is nicked at the near corner, a small vee, at the base of which a bread crumb stolidly resides.

"We should be open to all possibilities, shouldn't we?"

"I don't go for *that* one."

"I've just been . . . thinking about it."

"You were a better Catholic than I was," Tyler says.

"I was more cooperative, is all. And, you know, none of the priests ever molested me."

"Why exactly do you mention that?"

The smell of coffee suffuses the air, a mix of new coffee and the re-summoned burnt coffee on the metal disk that keeps the pot heated. There's a faint underlayer of last night's salmon. There's the kitchen's essential smell, which has shifted with the worsening of Beth's illness, though it hasn't changed entirely. When Beth was more able, it was piecrust (somehow the smell of piecrust dominated all the other cooking smells) and burnt sugar. Those ghosts remain. Under them, though, rising through like pentimento, is a hint of fried pork (a true ghost smell, they never fry pork) and the suggestion of male sweat.

"Now that it's all over the news," Barrett says, "I find myself wondering why no one ever messed with me, I mean it makes me feel like the fat kid I was. That's fucked up, I know."

"As long as you know."

"Some things can be bullshit and true at the same time."

"That, as you and I both understand, is ridiculous."

"Probably. But really. What exactly do you gain by being nobody's fool, ever? Do you actually benefit from the policy of absolute, no-holds-barred nay-saying?"

"I'm not sure I can have this conversation much longer. Not this early."

"Right. I'm off to work."

"Ciao."

"See you tonight."

"See you tonight."

D o you really like a mess?" Liz says to Andrew.

She's making breakfast for him, like a farm wife. It's a little sexy. It isn't *un*sexy. She could be a substantial woman, firm-featured, stirring the eggs in the iron skillet, living in a house fastened to a chirruping green vastness; a woman too ample, too sure-footed, for the winds to worry; smarter than her man, cagier, lacking perhaps his garrulous, two-stepping charm but possessed of a profound sureness, the depths of which he can barely imagine.

Andrew reclines on a kitchen chair, smoking, in briefs and woolen socks. If he knew how sexy he was, it would ruin it. Or does he know? Is he smarter than he seems to be?

"Huh?" he says.

"What you were saying on the roof. Sometimes a mess is part of it."

"Oh. Yeah, you know, I don't like to fight, but I don't back down from fights."

"Mm. I guess I mean, do you like a little skirmish every now and then, is it stimulating?"

Andrew, pay attention. I'm asking if I'm too maternal, too off-handedly kind, to hold your interest. Would you prefer someone rougher, someone more punishing, someone who disregards your feelings because she knows she's a treasure, someone who offers no apologies, ever?

"I got into a lot of fights when I was a kid," he says. "You know, when you move around a lot . . ."

They've gotten there already.

She plunks Andrew's breakfast down in front of him. He exhales a plume of smoke through his nostrils, drapes a muscled arm around her hips.

"You've always got to prove yourself," he says.

They've gotten there. With Andrew, any conversation leads eventually to reminiscence, though it usually takes longer than this. He's the most nostalgic twenty-eight-year-old in history. His past is his holy book, his seat of wisdom, and when a question presents itself, if the question is even slightly difficult, he consults the Book of When We Moved to Phoenix or the Book of When I Spent a Whole Year in the Hospital or the Book of When I Started Doing Drugs.

Liz plucks the cigarette from his fingertips and takes a drag, just for the sexy-momma-ness of it. Expertly, she flicks the butt into the sink.

"Eat, child," she says.

"You're not having any?"

"I'm still too high."

That's not exactly true. But now, right now, coming down, she prefers to be a hallucination she and Andrew are having together. Any demonstration of appetite would quell it.

He chows down, doggishly pleased by food. Snow taps on the windowpanes.

Before he can go on with the Saga of My Childhood Fights, Liz says, "When I was a little girl, I beat up everybody."

"You're kidding."

"Nope. I was the terror of the third grade."

"I can't picture you as that."

Picture it, sweetheart.

She strokes his cropped red hair, fingers the line of silver hoops in his ear, which inspires in her a minor spasm of fondness and pity. She knows where he's headed. She feels guilty, a little guilty, about knowing it, but what can she do? Warn him? Tell him how his blunt-faced beauty will erode; how the whole thug-saint thing works at twenty-eight, but . . .

She says, "You should never be the poorest person in the neighborhood. It's funny. My parents were so proud of our little house out on the fringes."

"Right . . ."

"Which, as it turns out, meant sending their kids to the good school, because they'd managed to buy a house that was within the district by about ten feet."

"And that's a bad thing?"

"No. I mean, suddenly I had teachers who weren't

drunk or psychotic. But suddenly there were all these kids who hated me for being a shabby, scrawny little thing. Suddenly I showed up wearing shoes that Dora Mason actually recognized . . ."

"Huh?"

"I went to school in shoes a girl in my class had just given to the church thrift store. Which was a surprise to me. I liked the shoes a lot, they were purple, with these little buckles, I can still see them . . . Anyway, I guess I'd assumed that my mother would by some magic make sure she hadn't bought me a pair of shoes that might have been the castoffs of the meanest girl in the third grade."

"Drag," Andrew says.

"A big drag. Dora naturally announces the truth about my shoes to the whole class. So I beat her up."

"You go."

"I figured, if I couldn't be popular, the next best thing was to be scary. Which actually worked pretty well."

Andrew grins up at her, showing bits of breakfast caught between his teeth. How is he not grotesque? It has to do with his innocence, his cluelessness, as fate forms around him, as the future arrives in such subtle increments it's as unremarkable as the daily mail.

"Don't beat me up, okay?" he says.

"I won't."

And, credible as a child, he returns avidly to his breakfast.

She leans over and places a chaste, kindly kiss on the top of his head. Here is the smell of his scalp, the . . . rampancy of it, its crisp, unperfumed vitality. There's a hint of product, some gel he uses (Duane Reade, an obscure pomade he must grab off the shelf because it's the least expensive one), but there is also that underlayer, the smell Liz can only think of as *growth*, no more preening or conscious than grass, and every bit as common, every bit as sturdily unquestioning. The smell of Andrew's hair, like that of grass, resembles only itself.

Eventually, he'll meet someone younger. Men do. He'll be tormented about it, there's not a trace of cruelty in him, which means she'll have to nurse him through his betrayal of her, bolster him, assure him that his happiness matters more to her than anything, which will, of course, be a lie.

And he'll abandon, soon enough, his already rather haphazard ambitions to be an actor. He'll come to his senses—he lacks the reckless courage, the delusional optimism. He'll begin to devise a new life for himself.

Which he will do without Liz.

In time, he'll get an actual job (*Andrew, it's already later than you think*). He'll meet the girl, the one Liz will not, in fact, have to help him feel less guilty about but the girl who comes along after her (or the one after *her*). He'll father the baby who'll mean, along with the wonder of a blinking, murmuring creature produced out of nothing at all, that he won't have the chance at a second reinvention. The money question won't permit it. This, man-child, is your invention, this woman and child, love them as faithfully as you can, because there isn't really anything else coming along, not at least for quite some time.

Whereas Liz, if she has anything to say about it (and she has something to say about almost everything), will be a staunch and rather intimidating old woman in sunglasses, gray hair pulled back tight, still making money, all the money she needs; still seeing boys like Andrew, harmed (there's no denying it) by her love for them, and so all the more bemused by their ephemeral conviction that they are the winners in the world, just as the farmer must discover, to his great surprise, that his heart will explode before he reaches seventy and that his wife will roll on for another thirty years or more, serene and majestic as the freight trains that have been sending their distant oboe moans across the dark fields for as long as anyone can remember.

After Barrett has gone, Tyler sings quietly in the kitchen. Beth will awaken whenever she does (is all this sleep a healing sign, is her system re-marshalling its assaulted reserves, or is her body just . . . practicing for death?).

This shard of hope . . .
This knife of ice . . .

Fucking song.

Why, Tyler wonders, does it seem so obdurately, so perversely and needlessly, difficult? He has talent. He doesn't aspire (not really, not deeply—well, maybe a little, at odd moments) to genius. He doesn't need to be Mozart, or Jimi Hendrix. It's not as if he's trying to invent the flying buttress, or crack the time-space continuum.

It's a song. All Tyler requires of it, really, is that it be more than three and a half minutes' worth of pleasantly occupied air.

Or. Well, okay. All Tyler requires of it is that it be better—a *little better*, please, just a little—than what he's technically capable of producing. It's the apple he can almost but not quite reach. Maybe if he shinnied another quarter inch up the tree trunk, maybe if he stretched his arm just a little farther . . .

There is, Tyler believes, a myth missing from the pantheon.

It concerns a man who produces something. Say he's a carpenter, a good carpenter; good enough. His work is solid and substantial, the wood well cured, the edges smooth, the joints all plumb and true. His chairs recognize the body; his tables never wobble.

The carpenter, however, finds, over time (time is always the punch line, isn't it?), that he wants to make something finer than a perfectly level table or a comfortable, welcoming chair. He wants to make something . . . marvelous, something miraculous; a table or chair that matters (he himself isn't sure what he means by that); a table that's not so exalted as to apologize for its modest object-life of load-bearing, a chair that doesn't criticize those who sit in it, but, at the same time, a table and chair that rise up, revolutionize, because they . . . what? (*What?*)

Because . . .

. . . they shape-shift, and appear in different forms to

everyone who uses them (Look, it's the table from my grand-
mother's farm! My god, it's the chair my son was building
for my wife's birthday when he had the accident, it's finished, it's here, how is that *possible*?).

Because . . .

. . . the table is the reincarnation of the father you lost—
patient and powerful, abiding—and the chair—gracious,
consoling, undeluded—is the long-awaited mother, who never
arrived at all.

The carpenter can't, of course, make furniture like that,
but he can imagine it, and as time goes by he lives with
growing unease in the region between what he can create
and what he can envision.

The story would end . . . who knows how?

It would end when a ragged old peddler, selling worn-
out oddments nobody wants, to whom the carpenter has
been kind, grants him the power. But this way it ends badly,
doesn't it? The wish goes wrong. The people who sit in the
chairs, who rest their forearms on the tabletops, are horrified
by their own conjured memories, or furious at these mani-
festations of their perfected parents, because they're so force-
fully reminded of the parents actually given them.

Or, once the carpenter's wish has been granted, he finds
himself imagining furniture imbued with still more powerful magic. Couldn't it heal maladies, mightn't it inspire profound and lasting love? He spends the rest of his days searching
for the old peddler, hoping for a second spell that will render
those tables and chairs not just comforting, but altering,
transfiguring . . .

There is, it seems, some law of myth-physics that requires
tragic outcomes of granted wishes.

Or it could end with the carpenter unenchanted. There's no peddler in this version, no bestowing of a wish. Increasingly aware of the limits of the possible, but lost to his old satisfactions, the carpenter finds limits to his joy in sanding and measuring, because a table or chair devoid of supernatural qualities will not, cannot, satisfy him any longer; because he has too vividly imagined that which he *can* imagine, but can't generate. It would end with the carpenter bitter and impoverished, cursing an empty wine bottle.

Or (hey) it could end with the carpenter transformed into a tree (by that peddler, or a witch or a god), waiting for a new, younger carpenter to cut him down, wondering if he'll be present, some essence of him, in the tables and chairs yet to be made.

Tyler can't seem to come up with an ending that satisfies him.

Back to the song, then. Try it, one more time, from the beginning.

To walk the frozen halls at night
To find you on your throne of ice

It's not really all that bad. Is it? Or is it maudlin, is it melancholia masquerading as true feeling? How are you supposed to know?

With a sense of guilty abandon, he turns on the radio. Time to get another voice into the room.

Here's the practiced sonorousness of a newscaster's voice, the baritone that's come to sound like truth, revealed.

". . . gathering momentum, it's going to be close, it all gets down to Ohio and Pennsylvania . . ."

Tyler turns the radio off again. It can't happen. Bush has not only killed multitudes, and murdered the economy. He's a manufactured person, the limited son of Protestant privilege, recast as a devout Texas rancher. It's a scam, it's all greed and mirrors, it's Doctor Wonder's caravan rolling into town with preposterous cures. How can anybody, how can one single person, be struggling to the polls (is it snowing in Ohio, in Pennsylvania?) thinking, Let's have four more years of that?

Is "throne of ice" just adolescent romanticism? Where, at what point, does passion bleed into naïveté?

Tyler is thinking about the word "shard" when Beth comes into the kitchen. She's like a Victorian sleepwalker, alabaster in her white nightgown. Tyler stands, goes to her as if she's just returned from a journey.

"Hey there," he says, draping his arms over the fragile bones of her shoulders, gently pressing his forehead to hers.

She murmurs happily. They stand, embracing, for a while. This has become a morning ritual. Beth may or may not be thinking what Tyler is thinking, but she seems to know that a period of sleepy morning no-speak is important. She's never said anything as she stands in Tyler's arms after awakening; she either knows or intuits that conversation will take them into a different day, they'll be two lovers talking, which will happen soon enough but is not what these first-thing-in-the-morning clutches are meant to be; is not this interlude of shared repose, this utter quiet, when they can still hold and be held, when they can stand together without speaking, the two of them, alive, for now, in the ongoing silence.

Barrett walks the snowblown street, trailing two feet of green plaid scarf (his one concession to color) that, released from the hunker of his heavy gray coat, twists and eddies behind him.

It's funny. When he ran through the storm an hour ago, wearing nothing but shoes and shorts, the cold felt enlivening, an ether that transformed him, like a man who falls overboard and discovers, to his astonishment, that he can breathe underwater. In boots and coat and scarf, however, Barrett just trudges along like anybody, a miniature Admiral Peary negotiating the ice field of Knickerbocker, no aspect of the fleet messenger about him, no wings threatening to

burst from his ankles, just a guy leaning into the wind, putting one heavy boot in front of the other.

The shop will be cozily unilluminated, free of trade, the
merchandise orderly and promising. It will be a sanctuary,
uncompromised until the doors are opened to the seekers of
Japanese jeans or intentionally wonky hand-knitted scarves
or an original Madonna T-shirt from the *Like a Virgin* tour.

Twenty minutes later, Barrett emerges from the L train
onto Bedford Avenue. The world is awake now. The corner
deli glows fluorescent in the snow. People walk bundled,
heads down. This early, Williamsburg is all commuters, men
and women with regular jobs, wrapped in pricey down great-
coats, in Burton parkas, members of the nomadic New York
tribe that colonizes the grim outer neighborhoods after the
younger and more reckless citizens have opened coffeehouses
and shops, as Liz and Beth did seven years ago, wondering
how insane it was to try to sell their particular offerings in
what had been a Polish travel agency, with a butcher shop on
one side (now a stratospherically expensive children's cloth-
ing boutique) and, on the other, a Goodwill store (which has,
over the past decade, been a succession of failed restaurants,
and is soon to re-open, at the hands of some new optimist, as
what appears to be a perfect replica of a Parisian bistro, right
up to its faux-nicotine-stained walls).

Even in its waking state, Williamsburg is quieted by the
snow, veiled and muffled, humbled, reminded that a mega-
lopolis is still subject to nature; that this vast noisy city resides
on the same earth that has, for millennia, inspired sacrifices
and wars and the erecting of temples, in an effort to appease
a deity who could, at any moment, wipe it all away with one
flick of a titanic hand.

A young mother, hooded, with a scarf pulled up to her nose, pushes a baby carriage, its small occupant obscured by a translucent plastic cover that zips up the front. A man in an orange anorak walks two fox terriers, both of which wear red booties.

Barrett turns onto North Sixth. There, in the middle of the block, is the brown-brick sternness of St. Anne's Armenian Church. He passes it every day. Ordinarily it's closed up, its windows dark and its imitation-medieval doors locked. Barrett's comings and goings don't coincide with the schedule of services, and it hasn't, until this morning, fully occurred to him that the church possesses an interior at all. It might as well have been solid brick, not a building but a monument, in the shape of a church, to centuries of Middle Eastern murmurings, to the recitation of prayers and the kissing of icons, to the imprecations and hopes, the baptizing of babies and the dispatch of the dead. It had not quite seemed plausible to Barrett that this stolidly deserted edifice might, at certain hours, have a life.

This morning, though, eight o'clock mass is being celebrated. The heavy brown doors are open.

Barrett walks up the short span of concrete steps that lead to the entrance, and stops at the threshold. There it is, strange in its way but also deeply familiar—the brackish semilight with its small glintings of gold, the priest and the altar boys (hefty kids, placid and rote, neither grotesque nor heroic, just adolescent schlumps—his own pudgy descendants), administering the ritual before an altar upon which two vases full of white chrysanthemums wilt under an enormous crucifix suspended from the ceiling, this one bearing an unusually gaunt and tormented Christ, who bleeds garishly from the wound in his greenish-white rib cage.

The scattering of parishioners, a dozen at most, and all, it appears, elderly women, kneel dutifully in the mocha-colored pews. The priest raises chalice and wafer. The faithful rise rather painfully to their feet (they must be subject to all manner of knee and hip complaints) and begin their trudge to the altar, to receive the host.

Barrett stands at the threshold, studded with the falling snowflakes that linger for a moment on his coat before vanishing.

Beth says, "I think I want to go to work today."

The rite of early morning silence has been observed. Beth sits at the table, nibbling an edge of the toast Tyler has made for her.

"You think?" Tyler asks. He's never sure, lately, whether to encourage her to do more, or less.

"Mmm-hmm," she says. "I feel pretty good."

Her tiny white teeth negotiate, without visible appetite, a morsel of crust. She can seem, sometimes, like a small wild animal, suspiciously but hopefully testing something unfamiliar that's been left on the ground

"It's really seriously snowing out there," Tyler says.

"That's part of why I want to go. I'd like to get snowed on."

Tyler understands. She's been especially eager, these past weeks, for whatever strong sensation she might be able to manage.

"Barrett's already there," he says.

"So early?"

"He said he wanted to be there alone for a while. He wanted a dose of total quiet."

"And I want to go out into the weather and the noise," she says. "We always want something else, don't we?"

"Well, yeah. We always want *something*."

Beth frowns at her crumb of toast. Tyler reaches across the tabletop, puts his hand on her pale forearm. He didn't expect to feel quite so incompetent at tending to Beth, quite so unsure about almost everything he says and does. The best he can manage, usually, is trying simply to accompany her as the changes occur.

He says, "Let's get you cleaned up, then."

He'll run a bath for her. He'll soap her shoulders, trickle warm water down her knobbly back.

"And when you're ready, maybe I'll walk you to the subway. Would you like me to do that?"

"Yes," she says, with an illegible smile. "I'd like that."

She's touchy about being ministered to. Treat her too delicately, and she bridles ("*I can walk up a flight of stairs on my own, thank you,*" "*I'm talking to someone, I'm fine, I like this party, please don't ask me if I want to lie down*"); treat her too casually, and she becomes indignant ("*I may need a little help with these last few steps,*" "*I'm exhausted by this party, I really need you to take me home now*").

"Eat your toast," he says.

She takes a single, game bite, and puts it down again. "I can't, really," she says. "It's very good toast, though."

"I'm widely known for my toast."

"I'm going to go get dressed."

"Okay."

She stands, comes to him, kisses him lightly on the forehead, and for a moment it seems as if she's the one who's comforting him. It's not the first such moment.

Tyler knows what Beth will do. She'll drape the clothes she selects on the bed, gently, as if the fabric had nerves. Everything she wants to wear is white, these days. White connotes virginity in some cultures, mourning in others. For Beth, white connotes a form of semi-visibility, a neither-here-nor-there quality, a sense of pause, an un-color, which apparently feels right to her, as if the assertions implied by colors, or black, would be inappropriate, maybe even impolite.

Barrett sits in the empty shop like a young raja, alone with his treasures. *Treasure* is of course a bit of a stretch—it's merely what Liz refers to as "merch."

Retail. Not exactly high art, not exactly the search for the cure. But still . . .

It isn't trivial. It may not be profound but it isn't trivial either, the little treasure hunt, the bodily satisfactions. The ongoing search, by Liz and Barrett and Beth (when she can manage it, though it's been some time since she's been able to manage it) for the genuine among the dross, for the small wonders—the paper-thin leathers and robust, ink-blue denims; the talismans on chains—that echo, in affordable (semi-affordable) form, the jewel-dusted scarves and talking books and articulated golden elephants that once were presented to sultans. The objects and garments that are made by people who might have been tailors or weavers in England two hundred years ago; swift-fingered, charmingly peculiar people who wake every morning eager to knit more caps or cast another silver amulet, people with something witchy about them, people who may in some inchoate way believe that they are producing not mere products but protective gear that just might keep the righteous warrior alive as he storms his way to the Grand Vizier's tower.

And, yes, we are creatures of the flesh. Who knows that better than Barrett? Who's better acquainted with the invisible fibers that tie yearning to vestment; those solemn parades of gold-threaded chasuble and starched white whisper of alb under the suffering wooden eyes of the crucified Christ? Doesn't the secular world want, need, to walk both proud and penitent, robed, for the benefit of some savior or saint? We worship numberless gods or idols, but we all need raiment, we need to be the grandest possible versions of ourselves, we need to walk across the face of the earth with as much grace and beauty as we can muster before we're wrapped in our winding sheets, and returned.

Barrett sits behind the counter, with his reading spread before him: the *Times*, the *Post*, and this tattered copy of *Madame Bovary*, which he is reading for the sixth time. He roves among all three.

There's this, from Flaubert:

At the bottom of her heart, however, she was waiting for something to happen. Like shipwrecked sailors, she turned despairing eyes upon the solitude of her life, seeking afar off some white sail in the mists of the horizon. She did not know what this chance would be, what wind would bring it her, towards what shore it would drive her, if it would be a shallop or a three-decker, laden with anguish or full of bliss to the portholes. But each morning, as she awoke, she hoped it would come that day; she listened to every sound, sprang up with a start, wondered that it did not come; then at sunset, always more saddened, she longed for the morrow.

This, from the *Times*:

Spammer Jeremy Jaynes, rated the world's eighth most prolific spammer, was convicted today of three felony charges, after sending thousands of junk e-mails through several servers, all located in Virginia.

Right. Searching for sails in the mist, waiting for the ship that might—might—arrive; scanning your computer screen for . . . the off chance, the insider tip, the gold that's been buried, all this time, right there, in the backyard . . .
And this, from the *Post*:

STONE COLD!
Two Nigerian women were stoned to death on charges of adultery, which is a capital crime under Islamic law.

Didn't Flaubert execute Emma for her crime? Yes, but then again, no. Flaubert wasn't moralistic . . . or, rather, he wouldn't have shaken his plump pink finger at Emma for committing adultery. He was a moralist in a larger sense. He was, if anything, writing about a French bourgeois world so stifling, so enamored of respectable mediocrity . . .

Emma was getting spammed, right? Adultery wasn't her undoing. It was her capacity for foolish belief.

This is Barrett's pleasure; his ongoing pursuit. Project Crackpot Synthesis. It's a mental scrapbook; an imaginary family tree, not of ancestors but of events and circumstances and states of desire.

He's starting from *Madame Bovary* simply because it's his favorite novel. Because you've got to start somewhere.

It does not, of course, lead anywhere. It accomplishes nothing. Still, he is, he thinks (he hopes), with this simple job and these un-sought-after, unpublishable projects, making progress. He's a shopboy, he moves the merch, and that's enough, it's exactly enough, to support and counterbalance studies that have no known destination, no future readership; that anticipate no scholarly discourse or rebuttal. It helps, too, that his job and his projects overlap. When it's time to open the shop (only twenty minutes to go), he'll wonder which Emma Bovary is bestowing ruin upon herself and her family by buying those three-hundred-dollar jeans, that vintage biker jacket priced at nine-fifty (even Liz is appalled by that one, though she's canny about what the market will bear; she understands the credibility imparted by stratospheric prices). It is, Barrett knows, a romance, and a perverse one at that, the whole notion of a house brought down by pettiness and greed. It's nineteenth-century. Citizens of the twenty-first century can max out their credit cards, they can extend their limits, but actual destruction, death by extravagance, is no longer possible. You work something out with the credit card company. You can always, if it comes to that, declare bankruptcy, and start over. No one is going to swallow a fistful of cyanide over a pair of ill-purchased motorcycle boots.

It's comforting, of course it is, but it's also, somehow, discouraging to live within a system that won't permit you to self-destruct.

Nevertheless. There's something about the courting of disaster, in shopping terms, that fascinates Barrett, that holds his attention, helps render him satisfied with his current stature. It's the technically extinct but somehow still plausible hint of calamity implied by the impulse purchase—the impoverished dowager or disinherited young earl who says, "I'm going to walk the earth in this perfectly faded Freddie Mercury T-shirt (two-fifty), I'm going to the party tonight in this vintage McQueen minidress (eight hundred), because the moment matters more than the future. The present— today, tonight; the sensation of walking into a room, and creating a real if fleeting hush—is what I care about, it's all right with me if I leave nothing behind."

It seems, to Barrett, like a harmless form of sadism, given that anybody who leaves the shop bearing that which they cannot afford is not walking out into the path of an oncoming train. And so he can enjoy, without guilt (without too much guilt) the suggestion that *Madame Bovary* and *Buddenbrooks* and *The House of Mirth* live on.

Barrett has lit only the modest lamp that stands sentry beside the cash register, shedding its modest amber puddle of illumination. Outside, dim figures negotiate their slow pilgrimages up and down Sixth Street.

Eighteen minutes to opening.

He is surprised, he is slightly mortified, when Beth turns her key in the lock, and enters.

She stands for a moment in the doorway's rectangle of snowy light. She appears to wonder, briefly, at the fact that she's there at all.

Barrett wonders briefly, as well. Isn't she still adrift in her ongoing dream? Isn't she supposed to be fading, gently and quietly, without a surfeit of fuss, back at home?

"Hi," she says.

Barrett needs a moment to say "Hi" in return. He needs a moment to receive Beth, once again, as a member of the living.

She's wearing what she wears, these days. The white do-rag (nothing so elderly as a turban) wrapped with exquisite carelessness around her hairless head; the white sweater over white ski pants; the white stilettos (in a snowstorm, thank you.)

Barrett returns to himself, sheds his aspect of the scholar interrupted, goes to her. She's shaking the snow from her wincingly fragile shoulders.

He says, "Hey, what are you doing here?"

She smiles bravely.

A dreadful admission: Barrett is growing weary of her courage, her efforts. They demand too much of him.

"I felt up to it, today," she says.

Barrett needs less than an instant to return to his ordinary, presentable form. He briefly embraces her, helps brush stray snowflakes from her shoulders and arms.

"In this weather?" he says. "There'll be, like, maybe three customers today."

"I felt up to it," she replies, and turns upon him a fiercely cogent, embattled gaze, like that of the half-starved child waving a banner over the barricades, the plucky girl detective who insists that the crime has not yet been solved, an expression he can only describe as the tyranny of the mortally ill: *I live now in a world beyond consequence or logic, I no longer do what's needed, I do what I'm able to do, and on these occasions, congratulations are always called for.*

"That's great," Barrett says.

Beth looks, with skeptical proprietorship (she and Liz started the shop together, it was Liz's money but Beth's aesthetic, her all-but-unerring ability to know what customers will and will not want), at the impeccably ordered, about-to-be-opened store.

"It looks good," she says.

And pauses. She was last here . . . Three weeks ago? Longer?

"Ready for business," Barrett offers.

Beth, dusted of snow, advances. She says, "You moved the jeans."

"Huh? Oh, yeah, they're over there now."

"They should be closer to the front," she says.

"Yeah, well. I sort of moved them. More, like, toward the back."

"The jeans are the building blocks," Beth tells him. "What's the most fundamental human urge?"

Barrett recites for her. "To find the perfect pair of jeans. To find the jeans that fit and flatter you so ideally that everybody, every cognizant being on the planet, will want to fuck you."

She frowns at his embellishment. The actual edict goes more like this: *Everybody's looking for the perfect jeans. Everybody's convinced that the perfect jeans will change their lives. Once they've got the jeans, they start thinking of accessories.*

Barrett volunteers. "We can move them back to the front, if you like."

"I think it'd be a good idea," she answers.

As it turns out, the mortally ill can be rendered more, rather than less, irritating by the authority impending demise confers upon them. Who knew?

After Tyler has walked Beth to the subway, when he's back in the comforting ordinariness of the kitchen, comfortingly alone, he lays out two—no, make it four—lines, and sucks them up. There's the tingling rise again, there are the neurons igniting, the ice-hot clarity.

Another droplet pings into the soaking saucepan. It is, it seems, an annunciation.

Tyler knows, he abruptly and entirely knows, that Beth will recover. The doctors still say there's a chance, and they don't as a matter of principle offer false hope, do they?

Beth will recover. Tyler will finish his song, and this one, finally, will be the one he's been reaching for, all these years.

He can feel the song, suspended over his head. He can almost hear it, not the tune itself but the buzz of its wings. He's about to jump up and grab it, pull it down, hold it to his chest. Never mind about feathers battering his face; who cares about pecking and clawing? He's nimble, he's ready. He's not afraid.

He'll be successful, finally, this coming Sunday, at the modest ceremony to be held in the living room. It's all so clear. Tyler will write a beautiful, meaningful song. Barrett will find a love that abides, and work that matters. And Liz. Liz will tire of boys, tire of her resolution to grow into a tough, colorful old woman who lives defiantly alone. She'll be willing to meet someone who can hold her interest for more than a few months, and that man will teach her about domestic deepenings, the modest reliable thrill of the familiar, which as almost everyone but Liz knows has been the way of human happiness since humanity was born.

After Tyler and Beth are married, after he's put out an album with a small scrupulous indie house, an album that attracts a modest but ardent body of fans (let's not get grandiose), he'll find them a better apartment in a less baleful neighborhood. Light will tumble in through casement windows, the floorboards will be smooth and level. And the American people (how could he have been so doubtful?) will not reelect the worst president in American history.

New Year's Eve, 2006

It's gone. It can't be gone.

It's gone, though. It has been, for months.

It will, in all likelihood, come back. It almost always comes back. Once a body has demonstrated its inexplicable weakness for lunatic replication, its hunger for annihilating growth, the habit tends to endure. The yearning for overproduction seems, even if forestalled, to fix itself in the body's memory, and what the body remembers most vividly, over time, is not cessation but rampancy, some ecstatic abandon (only the lizard brain understands about death), and so to that rampancy, that relinquishment of resistance, it will, usually, sooner or later, return.

But, for now, Beth's cancer is gone.

It's not just in remission. It's disappeared. Over the course of five months, starting a year ago November, the tumors began to shrink. It seemed at first like natural fluctuation, which had grown familiar. But then the tumors shrank a little more. And it seemed that the lesions on Beth's liver were healing, as well. Slowly. For a while it looked as if they merely weren't getting worse. But finally Big Betty, sitting in her office (the same office—the one in which the arctic whiteness was rendered all the icier by a framed Tuscan landscape print—where, three years earlier, the words "stage four" first entered Tyler and Beth's shared vocabulary), said cautiously, one lead-skied day in early April, her voice low and measured, that the lesions appeared not only to have stopped progressing, but also to be (Big Betty glanced briefly down at her desktop, as if the word she wanted were written there) healing. She quickly reminded Beth and Tyler that changes occurred, it was early to buy champagne. She ran through the litany of cautions and modest hopes and reversals, in the monotone of an old priest.

However, the tumors kept shrinking. The lesions healed. Even Scary Steve, the chemo guy, used the word "miracle," and he was clearly not the sort of man who maintained an inner vocabulary of magic or mystery.

Here they are, then, Beth and Tyler, on New Year's Eve, still in the Bushwick apartment (they'll move soon, Tyler is sure they will, but he hasn't broken through yet, the money's still not there). The living room is strung with colored Christmas lights. On the television, a DVD of a crackling fire in a fireplace. Dangling here and there, small green tangles of mistletoe, crisply unfresh by now, but they have to stay up until New Year's Day, it's a tradition, and the Meeks family (was it joyful rebellion, or just a general death of ambition?) has long been short on traditions. There was, always, a sense of improvisation, of cheerful underpreparedness, that Tyler would happily perpetuate, but which Barrett has put an end to. The Christmas tree in the Bushwick apartment was not purchased at the last minute, the gifts not hastily gathered the day before (which always resulted in strange choices, made because time had run out, and so, golf clubs for Barrett on his twelfth Christmas, in case he ever demonstrated an interest in golf; a blue-and-red ski sweater for Tyler at fifteen, when he'd been wearing nothing but black or gray for the past two years). For New Year's Eve, here in Bushwick, there are decorations, there are cheeses and meats and bread, there are candles, and a collection of tin trumpets, acquired by Barrett at flea markets, for the stroke of midnight.

With forty-seven minutes to go, Tyler and Barrett, Liz and Andrew are gathered together with Foster and Nina and Ping, all in finery: Barrett sporting the gold-embroidered vest he purchased at the Barneys after-Christmas sale (still, at 60 percent off, an extravagance); Liz in a short dress that glitters like zinc and shows, at the neckline, her collarbone tattoo garland of roses and vines; Andrew in combat boots, cut-off long johns, the 1972 *Dark Side of the Moon* T-shirt, sleeveless, that Liz gave him for Christmas; Ping arrayed on the sofa like the caterpillar in *Alice in Wonderland*, talking eagerly to Barrett and Foster and Liz from under the brim of a raven-plumed stovepipe hat only slightly smaller than the Mad Hatter's. Barrett and Liz pay polite attention. Foster (in velvet tuxedo jacket and rhinestone brooch) leans in, all avid-eyed attention. Ping, to him, is an elder who lives in a hall of wisdom.

Standing aside, talking to Nina, is Beth.

Beth has regained her luminous pinkness of face; she's gained twenty-three pounds ("Look," she said happily, last month, "I'm *zaftig!*"). Her hair is growing back to its full, former length. It seems, however, that Beth's hair, alone, bears the mark of her journey to the realm from which travelers rarely return. Her hair, once sable, once prone to languid curls, has grown back straight and lusterless, not gray, but not its former bright mocha, either. Its patina is gone. Beth's hair is acceptable, but it no longer curls or shines. It drapes. It looks neither alive nor dead. If Beth were a girl in a fairy tale (a fairy tale of a certain kind), her hair would be the mark of her battle with the witch, a battle she won but from which she did not return unaltered. Liz keeps urging her to have it colored, which Beth says she'll do, soon, but weeks pass, months pass, and Beth does nothing with her worn-out hair beyond rolling it into a tight little cylinder at the back of her head. She wants, it seems, a reminder, though she's never said as much. She seems to place some value on the mark left by the witch.

She stands in the middle of the room, one arm wrapped around the small of Nina's much-remarked-upon gymnast's back. Nina is stunning tonight, her strong rippling body draped in an antique ivory-colored slip-dress, her powerful neck hung with strands of pearls. Beth laughs at something Nina has whispered into her ear.

Tyler comes out of the kitchen (just a couple of quick, private bumps) and goes to Beth, who releases herself from Nina as gracefully as she'd change partners in a dance. Beth, coming as she does from lost Grosse Pointe money, has been schooled, she knows about dogs and boating, sends thank-you notes.

She kisses Tyler. Her breath is sweet again, no more trace of chemicals or lurking rot.

Tyler says, "So. Here comes 2006."

"You're going to be absolutely sure to kiss me first, at midnight, aren't you?" she whispers.

"Duh."

"I know. I just want to be extra sure that Foster doesn't cock-block me again."

"He wouldn't. You're a married woman now."

"And you're a married man. Which is the only thing you could possibly have done to make yourself even more attractive to Foster."

"Foster's interest," Tyler says, "in an unavailable middle-aged straight guy with no money will remain a mystery."

"Didn't Flannery O'Connor write something about how one of her swans was in love with a birdbath?"

"It was in her letters. She called it a typical Southern sense of reality."

Beth says, "That's Foster, isn't it? He's just visiting reality."

Tyler looks into Beth's bright, unmalicious face. There's no bitterness in what she's said, she doesn't mind that Foster is hot for Tyler; she insists, has always insisted, on living in the most generous and abundant possible world.

Tyler holds her. There's too much for him to say. She leans her head against his chest.

And, just that quickly, fear arrives.

Should they be celebrating like this? Of course they should. How could they do anything else?

But how can they celebrate tonight without anticipating some future memory; without wondering whether, on New Year's Eve of 2008, or 2012, or whenever, they'll be gathered around the recollection of 2006, when they, foolish children, partied as if Beth were truly healed? How might they remember this evening—these wild gratitudes, this soaring hope?

Still. Scary Steve, the chemo guy, used the word "miracle." What about that?

Barrett disengages from Ping and the others, picks up a champagne bottle from the coffee table and brings it over to Tyler and Beth. Barrett fills their glasses, raises his.

He says, "Happy 2006."

Beth says, "Happy 2006." They click their glasses together.

Tyler swallows his urge to say *Happy 2006? Do the names John Roberts and Samuel Alito ring a bell? Did the hey-that's-too-bad approach to Katrina make an impression? Does it bother you, even a little bit, that we're living through the SECOND TERM of the worst president in history?*

Tyler just smiles, sips his champagne.

What's wrong with him? Beth has been healed. He repeats the phrase, to himself. *Beth has been healed.* How can he expend even one brain cell on the new, right-wing Supreme Court?

Does Tyler really intend to grow into an old, righteous crank?

Barrett gives him the look. Barrett always knows. Tyler is thankful.

Barrett says to Beth, "Could I have you for a few minutes?"

"You can have me for as long as you like," she answers.

Tyler releases Beth. Barrett offers his arm, a gesture that's both parody of formality and not.

He says, "I promised Ping I was just going to check on people's champagne, and get back to this diatribe he's delivering about Jane Bowles."

Beth speaks softly, close to his ear. "Ping means well," she says. "Do you think he could be cured of the diatribes?"

"Tricky. They're not regular diatribes . . ."

"What exactly would a *regular* diatribe be?"

"They're not the hundredth rehashing of something he knows, they're not professorial, he just has these *enthusiasms*."

"He does."

"He makes some remarkable discovery, and he has to tell you about it. All about it."

"He's curious. He's the most curious person I know."

"Which is charming," Barrett says.

"Yes."

"And irritating."

"That, too."

Ping calls from the sofa. "Hey, you two, is it a private conspiracy, or can anybody join?"

Barrett and Beth hurry to the sofa, where Ping, seated majestically, holds forth to Foster and Liz, who sit like acolytes on either side of him. Barrett sits in the green armchair across from the sofa; Beth perches on one of the chair's arms.

Ping is declaring Jane Bowles the Patron Saint of Crazy Ladies, a conversation Barrett is eager to escape. He's long known everything about Bowles that's so revelatory to Ping, but Ping would be wounded if Barrett broke in—Jane Bowles is, for the purposes of Ping's immediate audience, his own discovery, a wild woman brought back from a dark continent, a marvel, found by Ping and now conjured for the wonderment of others.

In the interest of New Year's Eve, in the interest of a more general seeking-out of the kindness in himself, Barrett does his best to stifle a thought: *God save us from people who think they're smarter than they actually are.*

Foster, on Ping's left, listens raptly. Foster is looking for someone to be. He's spent his twenties and early thirties getting paid (both legitimately and otherwise) for the powerful Texas symmetry of his face and the genetic gift of his body; he's trying to decide what, exactly, to do, now that his features are growing a little too worn (always, the workings of mortality) to be marketable . . .

Barrett's worry: Foster is, at the age of thirty-seven, running around picking up anything that looks promising, with no ruling passion or overriding principle. He wants a new future, but is so disorganized in his pursuit of it that Barrett worries he'll still be figuring it out at fifty, still waiting tables, hiring out as a daddy on the Internet (*Are you looking for a real man? I know what you want. I know what you need.*) as he plots his course.

Some people probably assume that Foster's aimless search is true of Barrett as well.

Those people are wrong. Barrett is surprised to find that he has no strong or abiding interest in correcting the mistaken impressions of those who simply don't know.

Barrett is a humble shopboy. He moves the merch. And

in private, for his own benefit, he's compiling his Unified Field Theory of Everything, which, like so many projects worth undertaking, is doomed, and at least semi-delusional.

Start from this: the laws of physics that govern solar systems turn out to differ profoundly from those that govern the movements of subatomic particles. They should, of course, be the same laws—a planet should orbit its sun in more or less the way an electron orbits a nucleus. Nope. Surprise!

Barrett is not, however, to his regret, a physicist. He lacks that particular gift.

And so, he starts from this, instead:

At the end of *Madame Bovary*, Homais—the village pharmacist, the epitome of pompous mediocrity, a man whose "cures" only worsen his patients' conditions—is given the Legion of Honor medal.

Homais is of course an invented person. However. Among the medal's actual recipients: Borges, Cocteau, Jane Goodall, Jerry Lewis (it's true), David Lynch, Charlotte Rampling, Rodin, Desmond Tutu, Jules Verne, Edith Wharton, and Shirley Bassey, who sang the theme song in *Goldfinger*.

Among our American heroes—the women and men who'd be likely to receive an American version of the Legion of Honor medal—are surely Walt Whitman, Thomas Jefferson, Sojourner Truth, John Adams, Gertrude Stein, Benjamin Franklin, Thomas Edison, Susan B. Anthony, John Coltrane, Moms Mabley, and Jasper Johns.

But there's this, as well: Ronald Reagan is already being remembered as one of the great American presidents. Paris Hilton is one of the most famous people alive.

Barrett is trying, as best he can, to fit it all together. Starting with *Madame Bovary* and moving outward.

And he has seen a celestial light. Which has returned his gaze.

It's enough, for Barrett, to pursue the little way; to seek knowledge for its own sake. This, it seems, is the answer; it's the answer for him. He's a citizen of the middle realm. He is no longer tending bar at a failing Italian restaurant in Portland, nor is he scrabbling for tenure at some remote university. He sells objects to people, who are delighted by the objects he sells them. He studies in solitude and secrecy.

It's enough. It's just not what was expected of him, by way of a life's work. But really, what could be more depressing than delivering to one's audience the anticipated outcome?

And maybe—maybe—love will arrive, and remain. That could happen. There's no obvious reason for love's skittishness (though there is as well no obvious reason for the behavior of neutrons). It's all about patience. Isn't it? Patience, and the refusal to abandon hope. The refusal to be daunted by, say, a five-line farewell text.

I wish you happiness and luck in the future. xxx.

That from a man with whom Barrett had imagined, had allowed himself to imagine, the buzz of soul-contact, once or twice at least (that rainy afternoon in the bathtub, when he whispered the O'Hara poem into the man's ear, which was edged with fine blond down; that night in the Adirondacks, with tree branches fingering the window, when the man had said, as if sharing a secret, "That's an acacia tree").

You continue, right? You see an impossible light, which goes out again. You believe that a bathtub in the West

Village, on a Tuesday afternoon, has presented itself as an actual destination, not just another stop along the way.

This, Barrett Meeks, is your work. You witness, and compile. You persevere. You have, after all, made a significant discovery: The conjuring of a big splash, the building of a high-profile career, is not required, not even of those gifted with greater-than-average powers of mind. It's nowhere in the contract. God (whoever She is) does not need you, does not need anyone, to arrive, at the end, in the cloud field, with its remote golden spires, bearing an armload of earthly accomplishments.

Barrett sits with his arm draped lightly around Beth's tiny waist. Ping is saying, ". . . wait, this is the best line of all, Frieda, she's the respectable one in the novel, says, 'I have gone to pieces, which is a thing I've wanted to do for years.' How great is that?"

Foster says, "I'm getting it tattooed on my chest."

Barrett says, " 'To set the mind on the flesh is death, but to set the mind on the spirit is life and peace.' "

A pause ensues. Ping looks at Barrett as if Barrett has suddenly told a knock-knock joke.

"I'm sure that's true," Ping says with elaborate graciousness, as if helping Barrett cover up a faux pas.

Beth gently caresses his neck. She is married to Barrett as well as Tyler—the proof resides in a gesture like this.

"Sorry," Barrett says. "Go on."

But Ping's momentum has been broken, his riff undone. He smiles with the cordiality that must have been common among courtiers to French kings.

"Where exactly did *that* come from, angel?" he asks.

Barrett, glancing around, wishing he could liquefy, drip

away through the floorboards like spilled dishwater, or, barring that, explain himself, spots Andrew, standing idly nearby with a beer and a fistful of peanuts, behind the sofa, out of Ping's sight.

Andrew, placid and sure; Andrew, who, in the way of certain gods, couldn't care less about human squabblings; who literally fails to understand them. There are all these fruits, there's water and sky, there's enough for everyone, what could you possibly have to argue about?

Liz has kept him around for longer than usual, hasn't she?

"It's from Romans," Barrett says.

"As in, the Bible?"

"Yeah. The Bible."

"You're a marvel," Ping says. He's a diva but not a diva of the most vicious kind; he's a diva in the spirit of the grande dame, free with signs of his displeasure (witnesses must never imagine he's easily defeated, must not mistake his charms for panderings) but cordial, if coldly so. Nor is he is a pedant. He is merely a zealot, possessed of a fierce and singular loyalty to that which he's been given to understand as revelatory. Before Jane Bowles there was Henry Darger; before Darger the social career of Barbara Hutton. When Ping is in the grip, he's surprised, genuinely surprised, that anyone could be interested in anything else.

Barrett says, "Jane Bowles was probably being poisoned by the Moroccan woman she was in love with."

"I *know*," Ping answers, with fluttering, gossipy urgency. "Isn't it *amazing*? The woman was, by the way, an ugly old thing who went around in a black burka, and sunglasses. You should see the pictures. Here's Jane, lovely in an alabaster upper-crust sort of way, walking the streets of Morocco with a woman who might just as well have been one of the witches in *Macbeth*."

Foster's face—still spectacular in its pairing of carved-limestone Irish jaw with broad curl of lower lip, topped by that improbable, patrician, English schoolboy nose—goes slack with what might be amazement but which, Barrett suspects, is simply incomprehension.

"That's crazy," Foster says.

"Jane was crazy," Ping answers, with an expression of sated, feline satisfaction. He believes all great artists are, must be, if not deranged, eccentric, at the very least. Is that, Barrett wonders, connected to the sentimental little landscapes and still lifes Ping paints on the weekends? Does that explain his hats, his collections: the Victorian bird dioramas, the jewel-toned Arabian lamps, the first editions?

Foster says, "I guess I'll have to read her book," in a tone that manages to convey his genuine intention, and the fact that, for him, actually reading the book is an admirable but impossible ambition—he might as well have said, *I guess I'll have to learn particle physics.*

"It's not all gloom and doom," Ping tells him. "It's surprisingly funny. The lives great artists live and the books they write are two very different things."

Ping has his momentum back. He says, "You have to remember, she lived a very strange existence. She was an expat. She'd married that big fag, Paul Bowles, who ignored her, never sent her a dime, she was always broke. I suppose she lived in a world in which she thought anything could happen."

Beth administers a reassuring squeeze to the back of

Barrett's neck, gets up off the chair arm in search of Tyler. As she goes she says, "Twenty-nine minutes to midnight, everybody."

Beth's departure gives Barrett permission, too. He sneaks a glance at Liz, but she's gone genially blank. She has the ability to cancel expression, to sit in groups as if she were waiting patiently, with neither irritation nor doubt, for the hired car to arrive, to take her somewhere lovely and serene.

Barrett says, "Only twenty-nine minutes to contemplate my sins."

For Barrett, Ping's one true rival, wit is the only acceptable method for taking leave of Ping in mid-aria.

Ping puts his hand to his chest, in elaborately feigned horror. "Darling," he says, "you'd need twenty-nine *days*."

Barrett rises from his chair. Ping returns his attention to Foster.

"And really," Ping says, "if you're a deranged genius, why not go to pieces in a place where monkeys dart along city streets and vendors sell fruits you've never seen before?"

Foster glances, surreptitiously (Ping doesn't like wandering eyes), at Tyler, who extends an arm to Beth, wraps it over her shoulders, and pulls her in, shelters her against his sternum. Tyler. His handsome, lion-eyed ravagement. His capacity for devotion. Which is so sexy. Why do so many gay men lack that? Why are they so distracted, so in love with the idea of more and more and then more, again?

For a moment: Tyler removing Foster's clothes, tenderly, ardently, marveling at Foster's revealed chest, his furrows of abdomen; Tyler taking in the trail of darkish hair that leads downward from Foster's navel, as if Foster had grown the hair especially for him; Tyler hot for Foster but for Foster only, Foster's the exception, Tyler's not into men, he's into *Foster*, and he lowers Foster's jeans, paternal but sexual, ready to fuck Foster with the savage kindliness of a father, a fabulously perverse father, no taboos here, he's doing right by his boy, taking care of him, doting, knowing in the way of blood kin what it is his boy needs.

But Ping has continued. "It's better, really, to go out in a blaze. That's why we love Marilyn, and James Dean. We love the ones who walk right into the fire. I mean, Jane Bowles was hardly Marilyn or James Dean, to most people, but to me . . ."

Foster returns his attention. Ping is a good teacher, and there's much to learn.

.

Set free, Barrett finds himself without an immediate direction. Beth is talking to Tyler and Nina, and Barrett lacks the energy, just now, to enter an ongoing conversation. Andrew sits one-ass-cheeked on a windowsill, looking out at the night (or at his own reflection in the glass) as he chugs another beer (he consumes freely, the way an animal does, taking all the nourishment that's offered, as unconflicted as any creature whose earthly career depends on maximum intake balanced against minimal output). Apart from Barrett's veneration of Andrew—because of his veneration of Andrew—they are friendly, but in no way intimate. It would be impossible for Barrett simply to walk up to Andrew and say . . . something about hopes for the coming year. Or anything, about anything.

Barrett decides to slip into his room and lie down for a

few minutes. It strikes him suddenly as the most wonderful of all possibilities: the chance to lie quietly, alone, on his mattress, with the party playing, soft as a radio, in the next room.

When he enters his room, he leaves it in darkness, "darkness" being relative, without the blinds drawn—Knickerbocker Avenue sheds its mild orange radiance all night long. Barrett settles down on his mattress with a certain caution, as if he suffers an affliction of the joints.

His room, being white, absorbs the street glow, suffused by the lightly pulsing orange, a hint of the noir. The room is not unpleasant. But staying here, Barrett feels, more and more acutely, like an immigrant, come to a foreign country that is neither bleak nor verdant. It's the country that would have him, since he lacked the necessary papers for more promising places, and could no longer remain where he once thought he belonged; where his skills (the adroit skinning of an antelope, the ability to leach acorns into flour) have no currency or value.

The problem that marked his earlier years: almost everything is interesting. Books, in particular, to Barrett; and learning other languages, cracking their codes, beginning to see their patterns and their mutations; and history—the scraping away of all that accumulated time to find, still living, in its own continuum, a day in the market in Mesopotamia, where a woman ponders mangoes; a night on the verges of Moscow, the black air so cold it impedes your breathing, Napoleon somewhere up there under the same frozen sky, the gray Moscow darkness with its icy stars, which have never looked so brilliant, or so remote . . .

But there is, as well, the world of simpler aims, the fatigue at the end of a working day, whether you've been flipping burgers or shingling a roof; the love you can feel for the waitresses and the cooks, the carpenters and electricians, there's no other devotion quite like it (maybe it's a miniature version of what men feel after they've been at war together); the pure boisterous teasing mayhem of going out for beers once you've been released from your labors, *Willy has a crazy girlfriend and Esther really should get back to her kids and Little Ed has almost saved enough to buy that secondhand Ducati* . . .

Barrett, in his working life, was for so long the debutante who could not choose, who found every potential husband to be either more or less promising but never quite . . . never quite someone she could imagine seeing every day for the rest of her life, and so she waited. She wasn't all that proud, it wasn't as if she imagined herself too fine for any mere mortal; she simply found that her own body of inclinations and eccentricities didn't match up quite closely enough with the local prospects. It would be unfair, wouldn't it, to marry someone about whom she wasn't sure; and so she waited for conviction to arrive. She was still young, still young enough, and then—it felt sudden, how could that be?—she was no longer young enough, she seemed to be living in her parents' house, reading and sewing . . .

It's satisfying, in an odd and bittersweet way, that Barrett has found a career after all, and (strange, but true) all the more so that his career, as it turns out, is secret, has no worldly purpose, brings with it no possibility of wealth.

On the ceiling directly over Barrett's head, a Y-shaped crack has begun, every now and then, to shed a pinch of plaster dust, a sporadic drift of artificial snow, which means of course an argument with the landlord, but means as well that the building is dissolving (there are other signs—beams going powdery, an increasing aspect of ineradicable dankness), a view held only by Barrett, who's convinced that the building is losing faith in itself; that it can just barely manage the effort required of load-bearing walls and uncompromised ceilings; that one day it will simply emit a low creak of a sigh, and collapse entirely.

Beth, however, has been healed, her own crumbling reversed, and Barrett has yet to permit himself to imagine that the celestial manifestation, which occurred a full year and a half ago, could possibly be connected.

He can't bear the oddness of it. He can't bear the grandiosity. It's good to lie alone on his bed in his quiet room, with the party sounds and the street sounds drifting in, all those worlds going on without him. He floats on his bed like Ophelia, blissfully drowned (or so he likes to picture her): lost to life, yes, but lost as well to accusation and betrayal, more beautiful in death, afloat with her calm pale face and her white, empty hands turned to the sky, surrounded by the current-borne flowers she'd bent too far to pick; a once-troubled woman gone tranquilly to the natural world, given over to the bright movement of water, at one with the earth, as only the dead can be.

"Hey."

Barrett lifts his head, turns to face his open doorway.

It's Andrew. It can't be Andrew. Why would Andrew come and stand in Barrett's doorway?

But here he is. Here's his shape, the vee of his torso, the compact, shaven helmet of his head, the casual grace with which he stands, as if standing were part of a dance for which most of the population has somehow failed to learn the steps.

"Hey, there," Barrett replies.

"Are you holding?" Andrew asks.

Holding what? Oh, of course.

"No. Sorry."

Andrew shifts his weight against the doorframe, agile and authoritative as Gene Kelly. Of whom, of course, Andrew has surely never heard.

Part of it: the piratical uncaringness, that marvelous youthful conviction that if it were important, Andrew would know about it.

"Oh," Andrew says. "I thought you were sneaking off to get high."

Barrett forces himself through a dazzled moment— Andrew registered his leave-taking. But no. Don't linger there. Keep talking.

Barrett says, "You know, there's a remote possibility. Come with me."

He rises off his bed, takes the steps toward Andrew. Barrett has no dancer's walk to command. He puts one foot in front of the other. He hopes the word "hulking" does not apply.

Barrett enters Andrew's penumbra of scent—bottled, it could only be called Boy. There's the strangely unsour emanation of sweat (Andrew exudes nothing fetid, his sweat has no correlate or comparison, it is simply clean, and carnal, with perhaps the faintest hint of oceanic salt). No cologne of course, no deodorant, but a citrus something, a hint of juice and tartness; soap or lotion, maybe just lip balm, a lurking fragrance that's been purchased and applied.

Barrett exhorts himself, silently, to calm down, and experiences a brief, irrational fear that he has somehow said it out loud—that he has walked up to Andrew and said, out of nowhere, *Calm down.*

Is it a general quality of the besotted to believe that their thoughts can be read? Probably. How, after all, can such a turmoil of hope and fear and lust be inaudible? How do our skulls hold it in?

Andrew says, "I don't want to interrupt."

"No," Barrett answers. "I was just . . . I was taking a little break. Before midnight."

Andrew nods. He doesn't understand the need to take a break before midnight, but he acknowledges, he honors, the minor peculiarities of others. This, too, is part of his allure—his butch version of Alice's schoolgirl calm as she moved through a Wonderland in which nothing at all was familiar and everything was curious but only curious, never frightening or appalling.

"Come with me," Barrett says.

He leads Andrew down the hall, to Tyler and Beth's room.

The room is dark and empty. Without Beth lying in state, the room has transformed itself from treasure trove—filled with offerings to the sleeping princess—to junk haven. The objects have increased, but not substantially changed. There are more books, precariously stacked. The hula-girl lamp, still awaiting its rewiring, has acquired a sister, with a base shaped like a lighthouse and a shade emblazoned with sailboats. The skeletal duchesses of the twin chairs have been joined by a modest bamboo end table—a small, abashed-looking object, cheaply made, servant to the chairs.

When Beth recovered, when she left her life in the bedroom and rejoined the larger world, she took with her the
room's languid, Edwardian enchantment. It is now just a
bedroom, cluttered with books and castoffs, the den of hoard-
ers, charming in its way but a little nutty, too. Beth's dying,
the idea that she might do so in this room, cast a spell, and
now the room's silent denizens, its chairs and lamps and scal-
ing leather suitcases, are objects, only that, finished with
their brief period of transfiguration, returned to the realm of
the extraneous, waiting patiently for the world to end.

The bed, however, behind its barricade of bric-a-brac, is
blank and white, almost luminous. The bed is Sleeping Beauty,
the junk a thicket of brambles and thorns grown up to pro-
tect her.

Barrett wends his way among the accumulations. The
room may be an object-purgatory, but it is not subject to the
junk-store odors of dust and old varnish mixed with that
mournful not-quite-clean essence that seems to attach itself
to anything that has gone too long unwanted. Beth burns
lavender-scented candles now, in every room, the way an
aging woman uses perfume, to banish any detectable essence
of degeneration.

Barrett opens the drawer of the nightstand on Tyler's side
of the bed. The drawer is full of Tylerish stuff: condoms and
lube of course (Magnums, really?); a tube of some Japanese
ointment; a small pad of Rhodia paper and a Sharpie; an old
photograph of their mother (Barrett is still surprised, sometimes, by the reminder that she was buxom and heavy-
browed, with the skeptical, close-set eyes of a woman who's
never been overcharged by the village butcher; a handsome
woman, as they say, formidable, but not a great beauty, as

Barrett insists on remembering her); a few loose Contac capsules; a scattering of guitar picks; and . . .

The vial, protruding halfway from under one of the guitar picks. It occupies no position of honor. It is simply one more object in Tyler's drawer.

Barrett had hoped to find Tyler's cocaine stash. And hoped not to.

Of course Tyler hasn't quit. Barrett must have known. Right? Or not. He's been so long wedded to the habit of believing Tyler.

A strange phenomenon: there seems (though it's not possible—is it?) to be a confluence of secrets, suddenly revealed: a twinning. If Barrett is keeping the story of the light from Tyler, Tyler would naturally be keeping something from Barrett, as well. Balance must be maintained.

Which is insane. And which strikes Barrett as possible.

Another strange phenomenon: Barrett is pinned between his sense of betrayal (he performs a quick memory scan—how many times did Tyler actually *say* he'd stopped using drugs?—which matters because there is, it seems, a difference, for Barrett, between actual lies and acts that merely go unmentioned); his worry (coke isn't good for Tyler, it is not of course good for anyone, but Tyler, in particular, goes too edgily ecstatic on it, believes too utterly in his own hallucinated version of himself); and Barrett's own relief (of which he's suitably ashamed) at finding something that will delight Andrew—the pleasure Barrett derives from this minor criminal ability to provide; to be, for Andrew, someone other than a man without resources who's merely been lying alone on his bed.

Barrett takes out the vial. It's a small clear plastic jar with a black plastic lid. He raises it for Andrew to see. Andrew nods sagely, as if agreeing with a widely accepted wisdom that's been repeated, with no diminishment of its fundamental truth, for centuries. Barrett gives him the vial.

Barrett has done coke twice, at parties, years ago, and harbors no affection for it. It struck him, on both occasions, as little more than a self-imposed headache, accompanied by a greater-than-usual sense of anxiety and unease, both of which he possesses already, in abundance.

Andrew unscrews the top of the vial. He takes a ring of keys from his pocket (why would he have so many keys, there are at least a dozen of them), dips one into the vial, and extends the key to Barrett. On the key's tip, a neat little white mound.

Oh. Barrett had meant it as a New Year's Eve gift for Andrew. He hadn't imagined doing any himself.

What, though, was he thinking? From what train did he recently emerge, all gawk and polyester, into the glare of the city? Of course, Andrew assumed they'd do bumps together. That's what people do.

Barrett hesitates. *No thanks* is the simple and obvious response. And yet—eager little lapdog—he can't bring himself to refuse. He can't permit himself to be so . . . not-Andrew.

Barrett leans over, allows Andrew to push the key partway into his right nostril. He inhales.

"Harder," Andrew says. Barrett inhales harder. The coke is harsh and slightly numbing; medical.

"Now the other," Andrew says. He dips the key back into the vial, inserts it gently into Barrett's left nostril. Barrett inhales, harder.

Andrew scoops out two little mounds of coke for himself, one and then the other. He breathes deeply. "Nice," he says.

He sits down on the edge of Tyler and Beth's bed, like a swimmer who's made his way to a raft. Barrett sits beside him, careful not to brush Andrew's knee with his own.

Andrew says, "I needed that."

"Me, too," Barrett answers. Will he tell any lie, impersonate anyone, for the sake of mindless desire?

"Look out, it's gonna be 2006," Andrew says.

"Look out."

It takes Barrett a moment to understand that he's feeling the coke. There's a buzz in his head, a convocation of . . . not bees, exactly, nothing so alive; it's as if the buzz emanates from a flotilla of microscopic steel balls covered with bristles, whirling around in his brain, scouring away his thoughts and leaving only a stark, throbbing cleanliness behind. It is distinctly medical. *This won't be pleasant, but it's going to make you feel better.*

Maybe, this time, it will make Barrett feel better.

Andrew says, "Let's do one more. I mean, hey, it's New Year's."

He scoops out another small mound. Barrett lifts his head to receive it. He's worried that he'll miss, scatter it down his chin, but Andrew is as precise as a surgeon, he guides the end of the key directly into Barrett's right nostril, and then his left. Andrew does the same for himself.

"Nice," Andrew says.

"Very nice," Barrett answers, though it begins to be apparent that it is not nice at all. The steel bristles scour away. He can feel, he believes he can feel, the inner surface of his skull, ravaged, a white emptiness where his brain had been.

Barrett hears himself say, "Two-thousand six is off to a pretty amazing start, isn't it?"

It's only his voice speaking. He himself resides in a skull sepulcher, an ancient emptiness where some strange machinery emits its burr, metal teeth on metal teeth.

"Beth," Andrew says. "You mean Beth."

"No. I mean Michael Jackson getting off on those trumped-up child molestation charges."

Andrew turns his head, looks uncomprehendingly at Barrett. As, of course, he would. Andrew doesn't get it. Andrew doesn't speak sarcasm. To Barrett's astonishment, though, he doesn't seem to mind. He feels too twitchy, too nervously discouraged, to mind. Andrew, this is who I am. I'm prone to irony and wit. I'm not a great, accidental beauty like you are but I, too, cut a shape in the world.

The steel bristles have, it seems, abraded away his self-concern, his desire to be desired; he has only this voice, which speaks like some cranky oracle from the vault that was his mind.

"Joke," Barrett says. "I mean, yes, of course, Beth."

"I know, man. The body can pull off some crazy shit."

"It can."

"And, you know, doctors have *no idea*."

"Doctors have *some* idea. But they're not always right. No one is."

Barrett hears himself, wonders at his ability to speak in sentences. The mechanism is doing it, the small forgotten cleaning-machine that resides in his skull, doing the work its progenitors programmed it to do.

"If I got sick," Andrew says, "I'd go to a shaman."

A change occurs.

Barrett is surprised, but helpless. Some physical process, some assertion of the blood, seems to be announcing itself. Barrett's attraction to Andrew is beginning to fade.

The change has to do, it seems, with the word "shaman." It has to do with Andrew's insistence on it, despite the fact that Beth has recovered without having remotely considered seeing a shaman or a psychic or a layer-on of hands; it has to do with Barrett's own singular, visionary experience, which occurred in spite of his skepticism; and with hearing that particular word, "shaman," delivered in Andrew's New Jersey accent; it has to do with the very real possibility that Andrew isn't entirely sure what a shaman actually is.

Barrett has never spent much time imagining a future for Andrew. There was no possible future that might include Barrett, and so it was better, it was sexier, to dream only of Andrew in the present.

Abruptly, though, change is occurring. Barrett can for the moment see nothing *but* Andrew's future: Andrew an aging devotee of the improbable, living cheaply, doing some doltish job, turning by slow degrees from a perpetually attentive wizard's assistant into one of those men who consider themselves wizards in their own right; who get their "facts" from who knows where; who are well informed about the ongoing government cover-up of the alien landings at Roswell but can't name their state senators . . .

Andrew is an illusion.

Barrett has known that all along, known it since Liz first turned up with Andrew (she'd brought him along to a movie, was it *Star Wars III*?) and Barrett had gone hollow-bellied at the first sight of Andrew's frank and uncaring beauty, the nonchalance with which he wore it, as if he were the embodiment of some lost American ideal—built for labor, newly minted, his face pure and clear; Andrew the descendant of generations of men who rode bold-hearted off into unknown territory, into the mountains and forests, while the others— the cautious, the unsure, those who were grateful for what little they had already—conducted their various businesses on the sooty cobblestones of the East, careful about puddles and piles of manure.

Andrew is an ideal, an invention, a golden cup. Billions of dollars are expended annually, by countless members of the population, on the basis of how much or how little they resemble Andrew, the son of a New Jersey shoe repairman; Andrew who got it all free of charge.

Barrett can feel his interest waning. A balance has shifted. At one moment, Andrew's naïveté was the perfect, satyrly complement to his heedlessly perfect body. At the next, he's a foolish boy who will remain foolish long after time has done its work on the other parts.

Barrett says, "If you had stage four liver and colon cancer, a shaman could do exactly shit for you."

Andrew leans forward, looks avidly at Barrett.

"You don't believe in shamans," he says, in a tone of eager (flirtatious?) argumentativeness.

Is it true, is it possible, that Andrew has suddenly taken an interest in this new Barrett, the one who's losing interest in him?

It is. Any other response would be the surprise.

"No, I believe in, I don't know, almost everything. In the

right place at the right time. Magic is great, magic is under-estimated. But magic is not going to suck the cancer out of your body."

"Don't you think that's what happened to Beth?"

How exactly should Barrett answer that?

Barrett closes his eyes for a moment, letting his brain go electric, letting it continue cleaning itself out.

Then he says, "I saw a light in the sky once."

He's never told anyone. How could he possibly be telling Andrew?

Who else would he tell, though? Who else wouldn't question it, or joke about it?

And this new, dishonored Andrew, this Andrew who sits here, foolish and mortal as countless beautiful young men, over countless centuries . . .

"I see lights in the sky all the time," Andrew answers. "Meteors, planets, shooting stars. Probably a flying saucer or two."

Barrett says, "It was a big greenish light. Kind of like a spiral. I saw it over Central Park more than a year ago."

"Cool."

"Well, yeah, it was cool, but it was very strange, too."

"There's all kinds of strange shit up there. You think we know everything that's up there? You think we got it mapped?"

"It felt . . . alive. In some way."

"Stars are alive."

"It wasn't a star."

"Was it beautiful?"

"Yes. It was beautiful. And kind of terrible."

"Huh?"

"Powerful. Enormous. And then it went out again."

"That sounds very cool."

Barrett should stop talking now. He should stop talking. He says, "I've been going to church."

"Really." By the tone of his voice, Andrew apparently finds this neither strange nor ordinary. In Wonderland, the customs are unfamiliar, but not repellent. Alice simply wanders through it, polite and well behaved.

Barrett says, "I don't pray. I don't stand up or kneel. I don't sing. I just sit there, a few times a week, in a back pew."

"Churches are beautiful. I mean, organized religion is bullshit, but churches have holiness in them."

"Not this one. It's pretty plain. And it's just me and about a dozen old ladies, who always sit up front."

"Uh-huh."

"Nobody talks to me. I thought for a while that after a service, one of the priests would come over and say something like, 'What brings you here, my son?' But these guys are old, really old, they're just going through the motions and, I don't know, thinking about getting under the altar boys' robes once everybody else is gone."

Andrew laughs lewdly. He asks, "Why do you go, then?"

"It's quiet. It has an atmosphere, even this crummy old church. I just sort of sit there wondering if something will . . . arrive."

"Has it?"

"No. Not yet."

"Here you are."

Barrett opens his eyes. It's Liz, standing in the doorway, a reenactment of Andrew coming to Barrett's room twenty minutes ago. At the end of his life, will Barrett remember people standing in doorways, having found him in his various refuges?

Andrew says, "Hey, there."

"It's about eleven minutes to midnight," she says. She walks into the room.

"There is so much *shit* in here," she says.

"Tyler and Beth are collectors," Barrett tells her.

"Tyler and Beth are out of their minds."

She makes her way to the bed, settles in beside Andrew, who moves over to make room for her. Here, now, nudging against Barrett's side, are Andrew's right shoulder and the rise of his right hip.

It's sexy. Of course it is. But now that Barrett's devotion is fading, Andrew is turning from deity to porn. Barrett is relieved, and sorry. A ship is sailing off. Barrett glances at the lampshade, with its painted-on sailboats, the paint chipped away in spots.

Andrew says to Liz, "Want a bump?"

"And whose coke would that be?" she asks.

"I don't know."

"It's Tyler's," Barrett says.

"I've been under the impression that Tyler's stopped doing coke."

"Wrong impression, it seems."

"Whatever. Did Tyler say to you, please go into my room and help yourself to my private stash?"

"Hey, Lizzie," Andrew says, "it's a party, it's New Year's Eve . . ."

"Put it back."

Barrett says, "Everything here is jointly owned, by Tyler, Beth, and me."

"Not drugs. You never ever take somebody's drugs without having been invited. Put it back where you found it, right now."

Andrew passes the vial to Barrett, who opens the nightstand drawer and tosses it back inside.

To Barrett, Liz says, "You don't do this shit."

"Uh, it's a party. It's New Year's Eve."

Andrew says, "Barrett was telling me about this light he saw in the sky once. Over Central Park."

Of course Andrew would have no sense of secrecy. What could Andrew possibly imagine that ought to be kept secret?

"A light?" Liz asks.

Careful. Liz asks questions, Liz is not disposed to the miraculous or the inexplicable.

"Don't listen to me, not right now," Barrett says. "I have no idea what I'm talking about."

Andrew says, "It was this big sphere. It was beautiful and powerful."

"Barrett told you he saw a light in the sky," Liz says to Andrew.

"And Bigfoot," Barrett says. "I saw Bigfoot, over on Third Avenue. He was going into a Taco Bell."

Liz tucks her lips together, looks briefly at the ceiling, looks at Barrett.

"What was it like?" she asks.

Barrett takes a breath, as if he were about to duck his head under water.

"It was this sort of pale aqua color."

Liz continues looking at Barrett. Her face takes on a scrutinizing aspect, as if she were a detective who suspected

Barrett of lying about his whereabouts on the night of a crime.

"I saw a light once," she says. "Up in the sky."

"You're kidding."

"It was years ago."

"Where? Uh, I mean, in the sky, right . . ."

"I was up on my roof. It was early summer, I was living on the Lower East Side then, working in Joshua's store. I was going to bed, and I went up to the roof to smoke a joint first. Actually, come to think of it, I think it was opiated hash."

"What was the light like?" Barrett asks.

"Well, I guess I'd say a disk. Or a sphere."

"This kind of pale aqua?"

Liz emits a laugh with a strangely sour undertone.

"I'd say more like teal. I'm in retail, I don't see aqua."

"Tell me more about what it looked like."

She levels her eyes at him, a woman of patience, a woman sufficiently weary of overly ardent men that she's come to choose irony over irritation.

"It was this funny floating ball of light," she says. "There was something sweet about it."

"*Sweet?*"

"Yeah. I guess. Sort of like a satellite from the fifties. Like this little luminous has-been of a thing that had wandered in from some other time, when it used to be a marvel."

"That's not like the light I saw."

"Well, then, it seems we saw different lights."

"Did you feel anything? I mean, what did you think when you saw it?"

"I thought, This is really good hash, I've got to remember who I got it from."

"That's it?"

"Pretty much."

"What happened after?"

"I finished the hash, went back downstairs, read a book for a while, and went to sleep. The next morning, I went to work again. Do you remember what an asshole Joshua could be?"

"You didn't wonder what it was? The light, I mean."

"I thought some kind of gas or something. Isn't the universe full of gaseous elements?"

Andrew says, "Yeah, there are gasses and neutrinos and this shit they call dark matter."

"And you just went on about your business?" Barrett says to Liz.

"What did you expect me to do, call the *National Enquirer*? I was high, I saw a light, and it went away again."

Barrett leans toward her, his head close enough to Andrew's that he can feel Andrew's breath on his cheek.

He asks, "Did anything happen afterward?"

"No, I told you. Nothing did."

"Maybe not right after."

"This was years ago, things happen all the time."

"Think."

"You're scaring me a little."

"Come on. Think. Humor me."

"Hm. Okay. I found a pair of Jimmy Choos at T. J. Maxx, that's kind of a miracle, right?"

"Come on."

"You're very high, aren't you, honey?"

"A little."

"You never get high."

"It's New Year's Eve."

"Okay," she says. "I'll play. Let's see . . . it was at least ten years ago."

She pauses.

"What is it?"

"It's ridiculous."

"What is it?"

"It was, I guess it was, the year my sister came back."

The seldom-spoken-of younger sister. Barrett knows only sketchy details, after a decadelong friendship with Liz.

"Go on," he says.

"This is silly."

"Go on."

She pauses.

"She went off her medication. And one day she just . . . disappeared. For almost a year."

"You've told me that. I think."

"I don't talk about her much."

"I know. I know that."

"I'm not sure why, really. Well, okay, I guess it's because it obviously runs in the family, and I'm afraid it could happen to me. That's fucked up, isn't it? Like the Greeks refusing to name the god of the underworld, in case he overheard them."

"What is it that runs in the family?" Barrett asks.

"Well. Schizophrenia. It didn't happen until she was twenty-three. She'd been the smartest, loveliest girl in the world. She was fine, she was just fine. She was in law school, she'd gotten an internship with the ACLU, which as you may or may not know is a very hard job to get. And then she had this break. And she was someone else. She was paranoid and anxious about almost everything and she had these crazy ideas about corporate plots, and assassination squads and, oh, well, she . . . changed. She was just . . . another person. She had to quit school. She moved back in with our parents."

Andrew says, "Her name was Sarah."

"That was in fact her name," Liz says. "Anyway, she went on medication, and it helped, but only sort of. It made her a better imitation of who she'd been. But it was as if Sarah had died, and been replaced by some sort of pod person."

"I see pod people every day," Andrew says. "All over the place."

"She hated the medication, everybody hates the medication, it makes you fat and drowsy and it just kills sex entirely. And, one day, without telling us, it seems she stopped taking it. And left. One day. When our mother and father happened to be out of the house for a while."

"She left," Barrett says.

"She walked away. We couldn't find her. We tried everything. At first we looked around the city, and then we started calling the police and putting posters up all over the place. She was completely out of her mind, she was a pretty twenty-three-year-old, who knew what someone might do to her?"

"Women are kind of screwed, in the world," Andrew says.

"She had some money with her, we knew that. She liked having money, she'd just take it from our mother's purse, our mother never minded. We didn't even know how much, but probably enough for a bus ticket someplace. And after a month or so, I thought our mother was going to die. I mean, literally. Sarah left in December. If she hadn't been raped and murdered, she could have been frozen somewhere, she could have been starving to death."

A silence passes. The room crowds around them, all shadow and spike.

"I'd go over to my parents' place," Liz says, "and my mother would just be sitting there. In a chair in the living room. Just sitting there. Like she was, I don't know. In a waiting room, waiting to see a doctor or something."

"What about your father?"

"He was devastated too. But he was himself. He kept doing things around the house. Fixing things. Like, if the house was in better shape, Sarah would come back. I knew, I thought I knew, that if Sarah . . . never came back, our father would be okay. Fucked up of course, but he'd survive. I wasn't sure our mother would."

"Did you think she'd kill herself?"

"No, I thought she'd . . . vanish. Bit by bit. That sooner or later she'd develop some illness, something the doctors couldn't diagnose."

Andrew says, "People do that. People get sick from their lives."

Liz, her patience finally exhausted, gives him a stern, teacherly look. *If you don't know the answers, perhaps it would be best if you just listened.*

Barrett says, "What happened?"

"What happened was. Like, five months later, there was a knock on the door, and it was her. She looked awful. She weighed about ninety pounds and she had bugs in her hair and was dressed in things people had thrown out. But she was there. One night. Out of nowhere."

"Really."

"It seemed so impossible. We'd been hoping, of course we had, but we'd been practicing for the idea that she . . . wasn't alive anymore. And then one night, there she was."

"Where had she gone?"

"We don't know, really. She said something about Minneapolis, she said something about South Beach. But she'd turned down a law school in Minneapolis, before she had the break, and she'd gone to South Beach the year before, on vacation. We never really got the story. It was hard to tell whether she remembered where she'd been."

"She was home, though."

Liz nods gravely. She might be agreeing to some harsh but inevitable verdict.

"Yes. She was home."

"Which was kind of a miracle."

"I don't pray," she says. "I don't believe in God."

"I know that."

"But for a few weeks after Sarah came back, I did keep saying these silent thanks to every person who'd given her a dollar, every person who let her sleep in their vestibule, anyone who'd ever given her anything. After that, I always give a dollar to anybody who asks."

"This was after you saw the light."

"It was at least three months later."

"But still."

"Okay, yes, you fucker, in strict chronological order, it was after I got very high on some very good hashish, and thought I saw some kind light. Do you honestly think there's a connection?"

"I'm not sure. I keep wondering about that."

"Well. It's good, it's very very good, that she's home, that she's safe. But she's not *better*. She's back on her medication. She's fat and slow and she lives in her old bedroom. She plays video games."

"It's better than dead in Minneapolis."

"Still. It's kind of a shitty miracle, don't you think?"

Andrew says, "Hey, three minutes to midnight."

"I'm not really thinking miracles. I'm thinking, I don't know, portents."

"Two minutes and fifty seconds," Andrew says.

Liz tells him, "Go into the living room and make sure everybody knows. I'll be there in a second."

"You'll be there for the countdown?"

"Absolutely. Go, now."

Andrew rises obediently from the bed, leaves the room. It's Liz and Barrett, side by side on the bed.

"Does it matter?" Liz asks.

"Does what matter?"

"A portent. Something like that."

"You'd have to say it's interesting."

"Sweetheart. I'm thinking more like, I'd have to say it's wishful bullshit."

.

Tyler and Beth have ducked into the kitchen, for a bit of alone time. They hold each other, leaning against the countertop.

Beth says, "We're almost in another year."

"We are." Tyler buries his nose in the crook of her neck. He inhales her as deeply as he does cocaine.

There's a speck of grit in his eye. He tries blinking it out—he can't loosen his hold on Beth, not now, to rub at it.

"And the world hasn't ended," she says.

"Not for some of us."

She presses him more tightly against herself. "Don't start," she whispers. "Not tonight."

Tyler nods. He won't start. Not tonight. There will be no screeds about secret CIA prisons in Poland and Romania, warrantless wiretapping, or the fact that Bush himself has now admitted to thirty thousand Iraqi civilians dead since the war began. That would be the war against a country that didn't attack the United States in the first place.

Tyler says, softly, close to Beth's ear, "They found mammoth DNA in England."

"So, they can make a mammoth again?"

"That's probably a little premature. Let's just say they were never going to make a mammoth again *without* mammoth DNA."

"That would be so great. Imagine!"

"It would be extremely great."

"They'd keep him in a zoo, though, wouldn't they?"

"*No.* They'd want to study him in his natural habitat. They'd build a whole mammoth preserve for him. Probably in . . . Norway."

"That's nice," she says.

"You know what else?"

"What?"

"Fiji overturned its sodomy laws. You can be gay in Fiji now."

"That's good."

"*And . . .*"

"Mmm-hmm?"

"Princess Nori of Japan married a commoner, and relinquished the throne."

"Is he handsome?"

"Not really. But he has a true heart, and he loves her more than anything."

"That's even better."

"Of course it is."

From the living room, Ping's voice. "One minute to midnight!"

Beth says, "Let's stay in here, okay?"

"Somebody will come and find us."

"Then we'll tell them to go away."

"Absolutely."

Unexpectedly, Tyler starts weeping. It's a dry, quiet weeping, more like gagging on tears than shedding them.

Beth says, "It's okay, baby. It's okay."

Tyler lets her hold him. He can't speak. He's surprised by this sudden assault. He's afraid, of course he's afraid, on Beth's behalf—a remission so unanticipated, so inexplicable, could vanish as mysteriously as it arrived. They both know that. They discussed it once, and agreed to discuss it no further.

He weeps, too, over the wedding song he sang for Beth, more than a year ago. Why can't he seem to forget (never mind forgive) the fact that it wasn't a good song, despite the assurances, from everyone, that it was the best thing he'd ever done? Yeah, right. It was heartfelt, it naturally enough elicited tears, but Tyler knew, he knew, that it was more sentimental than searing. He'd been defeated by his own lacks. He winces, now, to remember: *sliver in my heart* had remained, but without any mention of ice; there may have been (he's willed himself to forget the particulars) *our double-handed, solemn approach*, rhymed with *the invisible driver of the ancient rose-decked coach*. He knew he'd run out of time, he'd run out of talent, and delivered a ballad, a nice little ballad, appropriate to the occasion, satisfying to all present, but not a creation hammered out of bronze; not a song that mingled love and death, that could be sung after the lovers themselves were dust. It was local. It was of course ecstatically received, but even as he sang it, as Beth stood trembling (frail then, her skin the same watered white as her silk dress), transported, aflame with love for him; he knew even then that he was a minstrel, his forehead encircled not by gold band or laurel wreath but plumed hat; adept at singing of love because he did so for hire, all over the county; convincing because well practiced, so accustomed to feigning romance for strangers that he could at this point do nothing *but* feign, even when the feelings were his own. The musical language of convincing fakery had become the only language in which he sang.

The song was lauded, as it would be. But the singer always knows.

Tyler weeps for many reasons, among them his own failure, a failure of the worst kind, a secret failure, as others insist that with his love song to Beth he broke through, he conquered, he found the treasure he'd been seeking.

"It's okay," Beth says again.

Tyler has not wiped that speck out of his eye. The petty distractions of the flesh . . .

From the living room: "Twenty, nineteen, eighteen . . ."

•

In the living room, a giddy nervousness. Where is everybody? It's just Ping, Nina, and Foster.

Foster, eyes on his pocket watch, says, "Seventeen, sixteen . . ."

Where, he wonders, is Tyler?

Ping asks, silently, *Foster, is tonight the night?*

Nina says, to herself, *I'm sorry, Stephen, I don't know what I was thinking of, I'll call you right after midnight.*

"Fifteen, fourteen, thirteen . . ."

Andrew walks in, doing his shoulders-forward walk, that simian thing. Why is he still here? How can Liz stand it?

There's no denying that he's hot. He's helpless, and she likes running the show. She's finally freaking out about her age. He must have an amazing dick. It's a maternal thing, she should have had a child. She's decided one of these guys is just like any other, why keep switching around? He's hot, very hot. He must bore her to death. Does she know she looks ridiculous with him? She must be getting tired. Maybe he's different when they're alone.

"Twelve, eleven, ten . . ."

Ping says, "Where's Liz?"

"On her way," Andrew answers.

Foster is ready, he's not a young thing anymore, I've loved him for so long. Why did I say that to Stephen, I've got to learn control. Tyler, where are you? Why did I say that, not young anymore, where are you?

"Nine, eight, seven . . ."

⋅

In the bedroom, Liz says to Barrett, "We're not happy, are we, about finding drugs in Tyler's drawer."

"No. We're not."

"You going to talk to him about it?"

"Yeah, I guess. I mean, I have to, right?"

"You'd be the one." She huddles into herself, folds her arms over her chest.

"We both saw a light," Barrett says. "You and I."

"An airplane. A little puff of cosmic gas."

"I don't think so."

"What else could it have been?" she says.

"Six, five, four . . ."

"We should go in there," she says.

"I know."

They remain where they are.

"Three, two . . ."

Barrett gazes imploringly at Liz.

"One."

.

Tyler and Beth kiss, ravenously. As they kiss, Tyler breathes into her and, at the same time, inhales her. They exchange some kind of potency, he can't tell whether he's kissing his own health into her or drawing her miraculously restored health into himself. It doesn't matter. He decides it doesn't matter. She's molded to him, they're here, it's 2006.

.

"Oops," Liz says. "Midnight."

"Happy New Year."

She and Barrett lean forward and kiss, chastely.

He says, "Do you understand that your first word of the New Year was 'oops'?"

"I guess it's another portent," she answers.

.

Ping and Foster and Nina kiss, rampant as children. Happy New Year! They embrace, as the sounds of shouts and firecrackers drift up from the streets. Andrew hangs back. Nina (*why does it always have to be me, why does everyone let the woman do it?*) beckons him over.

"Happy New Year, Andrew," she says.

"Happy New Year," he replies, with the bland unintelligent cordiality of an airline steward. He remains where he stands, close to the hallway entrance.

Why is he still here?

.

Liz says, "I should go find Andrew."

"You should."

But less than a moment later Andrew is there, striding through the bedroom accumulations like Godzilla in Tokyo. He is not, however, angry; he doesn't seem angry. He's just moving in a straight, unwavering line.

Liz stands. "Happy New Year, sweetheart," she says. She opens her arms.

"Happy New Year," he says, entering her embrace. They kiss. Andrew's hands cup Liz's ass.

"Happy New Year, you two," Barrett says, as he departs.

Andrew reaches over blindly, finds Barrett's hand, gives it a squeeze. It would seem he has that grace, that kindness, to offer.

It occurs to Barrett: Andrew waited, didn't he? He knew, he figured, that Barrett and Liz needed a little time, even as midnight rolled in.

People are more than you think they are. And they're less, as well. The trick lies in negotiating your way between the two.

Barrett passes the kitchen on his way to the living room. Tyler and Beth are making out. Should he pass discreetly by? No, who cares, he's family, he's Beth's backup husband, he has the rights of interruption.

"Happy New Year," he says.

They disengage, slightly stunned, as if they were surprised to find themselves in this kitchen, in this world.

"Happy New Year, baby," Beth says. She comes to Barrett, wraps her thin arms around his shoulders, gives him a proper kiss.

Tyler steps over as well, puts his arms around both of them, with Beth in the middle, pressed between Tyler and Barrett. Barrett is all the more aware of her tiny, creaturely aspect, the resilient small-bonedness of her. She is at the moment a white mouse, a cherished pet, held tenderly but held, nevertheless, by two men who could crush her if they chose to. Barrett could swear he feels her quivering, as a mouse might, held in one's hands—that minute ongoing tremble that's part of a mouse's physical being; due to a perpetual state of guarded fearfulness (you are after all a prey animal) but also simply the manifestation of smallness, of a fast-beating heart the size of a blueberry.

Barrett says to Tyler, "If you say 'group hug,' I'll smack you."

Tyler reaches over, runs his fingers through Barrett's hair. Beth stands quietly between them, rocking ever so slightly from side to side. She lifts her head, leans the back of her neck against Tyler's chest. Her eyes are closed.

Barrett can feel her, summoning something. It's palpable. It prickles across her skin.

She says, "I entered death."

"No," Barrett says. "You didn't."

Beth doesn't open her eyes. There's an aspect of recitation; of a speech long memorized that must now, finally, be delivered.

"I don't mean actually," she says. "But something changed."

"Earth language, please," Barrett says.

"Mm. Okay. For a long time, I was a sick person. And then. There was some kind of shift."

For a moment, Tyler's breathing is the loudest sound in the room.

Beth says, "I sort of. Well. I started to die. I embarked on something. And it was different. I was still sick. I still felt awful. But. I'd felt like a healthy person who got sick. And then. I was a sick person, I couldn't remember being anything else. It was like the lights started to go off. The way you turn off the lights in a house when everybody's going to bed."

Nobody speaks. Shouldn't someone ask a question?

"What did it feel like?" Barrett asks.

"Not good. But not really exactly bad, either. There was just this sort of. Dim nowhere. It didn't really exactly matter if it was good or bad. That wasn't really the question."

She continues to rest her head against Tyler's chest. Her eyes remain closed.

"A dim nowhere," Barrett says, because Tyler, it seems, can't be counted on just now.

"Does that make sense?" she asks.

"Kind of."

"I want you to know. That it wasn't so terrible. I want you to know that."

"We do," Tyler says.

"Because," she adds, "there isn't all that much time."

"In life, you mean?" Barrett says. "For any of us?"

She rolls her head slightly from side to side against the square fleshly plate of Tyler's pectoral muscle.

"Yes," she says. "I guess that's what I mean."

.

At ten minutes past midnight they're all in the living room, wondering what to do next.

Foster shouts, "Predictions for 2006!"

Which is, of course, a mistake. Everyone does not look at Beth.

Beth says, without hesitation, "I predict a great night tonight."

They raise their glasses. There are whoops and cheers.

Yes, Barrett thinks once again, this is why Tyler loves you so. It's another of the old stories, replayed: the simple girl who ascends to some throne or other and becomes legendary, in part because she brings kindness and other ordinary human virtues to a realm more generally ruled by deviousness, by cruelties both petty and annihilating.

A silence settles. Discomfort has not yet left the room.

Foster rages through his own mind, wondering if he can offer something to counterbalance his clumsiness, or if speaking again will only make it worse. Tyler must consider him thoughtless and callous, now. Tyler will never permit that hour of abandon . . .

Tyler says, "I predict that John Roberts will receive instructions from God Himself to be a better man. Human rights will flourish. Women and gays and people of color will stop worrying. Dances will be danced in streets across the nation."

There are more cheers and whoops, another raising of glasses.

For the first and possibly last time in his life, Tyler has made a roomful of people grateful for his implied insistence that nobody but he takes things quite sufficiently seriously; for the habit that's earned him the nickname Mister No Fun (by which he is rendered, every time he hears it, simultaneously embarrassed and proud).

Barrett says, "I predict that black will *still* be the new black."

Liz adds, "And pink will always be the navy blue of India."

Barrett puts an arm over Liz's shoulders. She plants a quick kiss on his cheek. They have not, thank God, lost their capacity for triviality.

·

The little party unfurls. Foster, Nina, and Ping all leave at the same time, as if there existed some clear if unspoken shared understanding that the moment of departure has arrived. The bell has been rung, the carriages called, and nobody wants to be the one who lingers overlong; who misses the cue; the one of whom it might be said, just after the door closes, *I thought he'd never leave.*

Foster, Ping, and Nina say their goodbyes to one another, out on Knickerbocker. *Happy New Year, darling, love you, this was such a lovely night, you win the prize for best hat, safe travels, I'll call you tomorrow.*

Nina goes north, Ping and Foster south.

Nina is going to Red Hook, to see if she can patch things up with her boyfriend (*Baby, I panicked, I think I'm falling in love with you and it scares me, you know how I am about losing control*), which will hold them together for another couple of months, until Nina falls in love with a surgeon she meets at Barneys (*Nina, the bold and audacious: "Honey, I don't mean to be nosy, but don't buy that sweater, white people should never wear yellow"*); a man who obeys her on the subject of the sweater but never obeys her again; a man so certain that Nina is beautiful, but unqualified in any realm of thought and action that does not involve apparel (*that's my Nina, she's got seventy-one pairs of shoes, guess what she pays for that haircut*), that she will retract most of her opinions when challenged (*oh, well, I really don't know all that much about it*); she'll grow her hair long (*a woman with long hair is just sexier, okay?*) and put on a few pounds (*a woman should have an ass*); she'll drift away from her friends (*that pack of losers*); she'll live with the surgeon in a doorman building on the Upper West Side.

Ping will walk Foster to the L train, say goodbye to him there with a quick, French-style kiss on either cheek. As Foster descends the subway stairs, Ping will imagine him headed to a disco out of Kubla Khan: gently pulsing, grotto-like (for some reason, in Ping's mind, the dance floor is circled by a clear blue moat, where beautiful boys float languidly in little silver boats). Once Foster is out of sight, Ping will call a car service (feeling ever so slightly guilty for the fact that he can afford it). The comeuppance he desires will, however, arrive quickly enough: the car will take almost forty-five minutes to arrive. The dispatcher has reminded him about the slow-down caused by New Year's Eve, but still, *forty-five minutes?* As Ping waits on Morgan Avenue, which is as desolate as certain outlying neighborhoods in Kraków must be, even on this most celebratory of nights, he'll think, with increasing fondness, as the car does not and does not arrive, of his small but comfortable rent-controlled apartment on Jane Street (*Why would anyone live in Bushwick?*) as, by way of holiday observation, a windblown plastic bag that says Merry Xmas scutters by; he'll feel like the weary traveler he is, longing to be in bed (a sleigh bed from the late 1800s, bought for almost nothing at that little place in New Bedford); the gem-studded Arabian lamp lit; reading Jane Bowles. He'll be grateful for the small fortune that's been granted him. He'll tell himself that he's lucky, that he's blessed.

Foster will go to a club, an enormous black-walled room that does not in any way resemble Ping's vision of ethereal fecundity; a dark room full of men dancing, with their shirts off, to house music. Foster, still cringing with embarrassment about having lost his chance with Tyler, will pick up an easy and inconsequential boy named Austin, a starved-looking, avid, fox-faced man-child, no one's idea of a prize. It's a punishment Foster visits upon himself. Which will render it all the more surprising when, the following morning, the boy mentions his last name—Mars. He's an heir to a chocolate fortune. This will continue to surprise Foster, albeit with ever-diminishing force, when he finds himself, ten years later, living with Austin Mars on a horse farm in West Virginia.

Not long after Ping, Nina, and Foster have departed, Liz and Andrew go home as well. Barrett, Tyler, and Beth sit together on the couch, the big saggy matronly couch that is Tyler and Barrett's sole remaining inheritance from their mother (their father took pretty much everything else, moved it all to Atlanta). The couch is covered with blankets and Indian tapestries (you don't want to know about its nubbled, corpse-colored upholstery). The couch, in its decrepitude, receives you, holds you, gives under the weight of you, takes you in.

Barrett says, "What do you think of 2006 so far?"

"Seems all right," Tyler answers.

"Nothing terrible has happened yet."

"Not to us," Tyler says. "Not to white people with an apartment and a fire crackling away on the TV . . ."

Beth puts a finger to his lips.

He stops talking.

Barrett will understand, afterward, why that moment, that tiny gesture, feels revelatory. It will take him a while.

The yet-to-come realization: Tyler is Beth's, now. Now that Beth has been restored to health, they're a couple in a way they were not, when Beth was dying. The Beth who was slipping away, the Beth who required more and more attentions and ministrations, had been both Tyler's and Barrett's: their flickering saint, their runaway princess who was being reclaimed, hour by hour and day by day, by the sorceress from whom she'd thought she'd escaped.

Tyler and Barrett were her attendants. They were Team Beth.

But now, tonight, New Year's Eve 2006, Beth has

declared herself to be Tyler's wife, and has done so by the simplest and most economical of means: she's put a finger to his lips, and shut him up.

Which Tyler would not, could not, permit Barrett to do.

Tyler has never been silenced by Barrett. It's not part of their brother pact. They are permitted endless discussion, which may or may not lead to argument. It's fine if they talk over each other, if they vie and joust and jest and mull and corroborate, but Beth can put a stop to it, with one tiny finger, as easily as she'd switch off a lamp.

And it's Beth's job, now, to talk to Tyler about his drug relapse. It's become her province; it's no longer a duty Barrett is compelled to perform. Barrett and Tyler aren't married anymore.

These ideas will arrive later. Now, on the sofa, a little less than an hour into the New Year, all Barrett knows is that he has to get up, kiss them both good night, and go to bed in his own room.

"Good night, sweethearts."

"Good night, my love."

"Sweet dreams."

"See you in the newness of tomorrow."

"See you in hell, motherfucker."

"Good night, good night, good night."

.

After Barrett has gone to bed, Tyler says to Beth, "This is our only New Year's resolution. We're moving out of this dump by 2007."

"It'd be nice to move," Beth says. "I'm okay here, though. I like this place."

"Imagine something less dreary, though."

"Who doesn't want less dreary?"

"Imagine no more acoustic ceiling. No more shag carpet."

"It'd be nice, no denying it."

"Imagine a neighborhood where you could walk down the block and get actual produce. Fresh vegetables, baby. A mere block or two away."

"Would Barrett be moving, with us?" she asks.

Tyler pauses. It would seem that the question hasn't occurred to him. He gazes, briefly, into the televised fire.

"I don't know," he says. "What do you think?"

She says, "You're going to do it to me, aren't you?"

"Uh, do what, exactly?"

"You want me to be the wife who says, Your brother's got to move out."

"Earth to Beth."

"I'm serious."

"Okay," he says. "Do you *want* Barrett to move out?"

"No. I don't know. What I want is for you not to expect me to bring it up."

"This is silly."

"Not to me."

"I mean, it's New Year's Eve, we had a great party, we're going to argue about a new apartment we don't have yet?"

Beth gets up off the sofa. "I'd like to go out for a little. Just for a walk."

Tyler stands too. "You're mad?"

"Not really. I'm just going for a walk, okay?"

He puts his arms around her shoulders, draws her in. She does not resist, but neither does she yield.

He says, "I want to make you happy. That's all."

"Maybe you should stop. Trying to make me happy, all the time."

"That's an unusual request."

She pulls out of his embrace. "It's nothing. It's no big deal. I'll go for a little walk, and I'll be fine again. All right?"

"I'm not crazy about the idea of you going out there alone, at this hour."

"It's New Year's Eve. There'll be people."

"Drunk people. Aggressive and dangerous people."

"I'll be back in, like, twenty minutes."

"Wear your fleece coat, it's cold out."

"I *know* it's cold. I'm going to wear my fleece coat."

"This is a little strange. What seems to be happening, here."

"We're having a fight. That's all it is. We're going to have fights, sometimes."

"I know."

"Do you?"

"Go for a walk."

"I am."

And yet, she doesn't move, not right away. She and Tyler stand quietly together for a moment, as if they were waiting. For something. For someone. For an announcement. For news.

•

After Beth has left the apartment, Tyler sits alone on the sofa (the sofa is, by now, as much dog as furniture). The Christmas lights are still lit (there is no red quite as beautiful to Tyler as the particular red of an illuminated Christmas-tree bulb). The DVD of the fireplace still crackles on the TV screen.

This surprise: Beth, restored to health, is his wife. They're married, in the same way any two people are married. There are bickerings. There are irritations.

What, Tyler asks himself, did he expect?

Transcendence, maybe. An endless loving innocence, after the beast has been slain; a future polished to a brilliant, perfect shine because it's been so unexpectedly granted.

Don't something like half the people who win the lottery end up killing themselves? Something like that.

Tyler's knowledge that he's being absurd doesn't seem to help as much as it should.

Alone, he's more alert to the noises that sift in from the street. The shouts, the crowings of Happy New Year, the joyful bleating of horns and the occasional furious blast (how can a car horn, which makes one sound only, be so identifiably either rageful or glad?), the distant booms of fireworks, which Tyler can hear but not see.

Two thousand six. The world is fucked.

Semi-fucked. Pre-fucked.

Tyler has admitted to himself (he tries to submit to his own thoughts and deeds the same scrutiny he brings to the larger world) that while he is of course relieved, he's also ever so slightly disappointed that more shit isn't hitting more fans, more immediately. We (the lucky few, remember) still live comfortably, two years into the second term. We have not come home to find our apartments ransacked; we have not been taken into underground rooms and had our heads shaven.

Still. Tyler wants to have been more right. He persists

in a particular fantasy: he and Barrett (he can't bring himself to include Beth) are in an endless line of people, being taken . . . somewhere. Barrett apologizes for the mildness of his passion, that November in 2004, and Tyler consoles him, forgives him, assures him that he could not possibly have known, for which Barrett is touchingly grateful.

Ahead of them in line is an older couple, still wearing what's left of their jewels and Armani. They whisper to each other that there's clearly been a mistake; they reassure each other that it will soon be rectified, and Tyler finally, finally gets to let somebody have it; he gets to do more than rage at the *Times* (thanks for the apology on the editorial page, *New York* Fucking *Times*, about having been perhaps ever so slightly hasty when you slanted the news to help promote the war); more than call in to that radio program—which he did exactly once, having realized that, instead of a voice of calm severity, of heroic and profound humanness, he'd sounded like just another one of the nut jobs who rant on radio call-in programs. He's free of the restraint he practices with his brother and his wife and his friends, who have always been on his side, who agree with him on every subject, who can only be chastised for failing to do . . . what, exactly? Organize? Get petitions signed? Be as vitriolic as he?

That's it. That's really it. He wants everyone he knows to be as upset and vitriolic as he is. He's tired of feeling so alone.

But here, now, in Tyler's fantasy, are the culprits themselves: the ones who prospered, who thought of no one and nothing beyond themselves, who pulled the lever on Election Day thinking, Yes, this is working,

Here they are, this once-prosperous couple, shocked, altered, dragged before the seat of the conqueror who'd promised it was only the servants and petty thieves who'd suffer. Here they are, faced with the consequences, and finally, Tyler can lay into them.

The fantasy, however, always ends there, with the eye contact, the shared realization, the abashment on those well-fed faces. Tyler doesn't think about his actual screed. If this were one of his sexual fantasies, the moment of righteous revelation would be the moment at which he came. In his sex dreams, the moment she spreads her tits over his face or rolls her own panties onto him or hikes her legs up over his shoulders is the moment he always lets it go.

He is, it seems, all about anticipation. That's something to think about.

Not now, though. Now he's in his living room, in his own skin, drifty on champagne and coke, too comfortable (forgive him) to dwell on the fact that his white skin has bought it all.

He permits himself to drift . . .

And drifts, unexpectedly, onto a slick of gratitude for these minutes alone, because (stop this) he's occasionally nostalgic for the days when Beth was ill, when his purpose was as compact and unwavering as a surface-to-air missile.

It seems that this would be a good time for another bump or two. He's cut down, he's cut way down, but a bump (or two) would be good right now; it would help him with his shame at the fact that he harbors even a wisp of nostalgia for the days of Beth's illness; for the singularity and purpose they conferred; and yes, even for the stern granite face of mortality itself, against which he could rage. How fucked up is *that*? How fucked up is it that his songwriting feels even more swampily amorphous now; that without the race against time, without the need to have something miraculous to give his lover while she was still present to receive it . . . his sense of purpose has gone shifty on him?

Enough. He can give himself a break. A short break, tonight. He gets up to go to the bedroom for his vial. After all, it's New Year's Eve.

Beth walks out onto Knickerbocker. A bright, crystalline snow has started falling, fine enough to be all but invisible save for the orange nimbuses shed by the streetlights, little movies that show themselves, one per block—gentle flurries of orange-gold sparkle, a special effect, projected onto the streetlights' small circles of shine.

There are people on the street, a few people, which qualifies as a crowd on Knickerbocker, which, every other night, is disquietingly empty. People are coming home from whatever other neighborhood offers more in the way of lights and music. Up ahead, at the end of the block, three Hispanic girls walk unsteadily, arm in arm, spike-heeled, happy-looking but depleted, having reached the far end of a night that started hours ago, when they tried dress after dress, did one another's makeup, composed one another's hair, imagined (or refused to imagine) that tonight might be the night he turns up at a club or party, the night he sees her as ravishing as she has it in her to be; that tonight could take her eventually to a house somewhere, her little boy asking to be allowed one more dish of ice cream, her baby girl asleep in her arms as she tells someone, *Yeah, we met on New Year's Eve, how corny is that?*

It's remarkable, being alive. Being, once again, someone walking through a dust of blowing snow, passing the window of the liquor store, which offers an array of bottles surrounded by tiny blinking lights; seeing her own reflection skim across the glass; being, once again, able to receive the ordinary pleasures, boots on pavement, hands in the pockets of her jacket, feeling in the right-hand pocket what must be an old Tic-Tac, fingering it, walking along.

She walks, without much purpose, for a couple of blocks, as far as Flushing Avenue, feeling the sting of the cold in her lungs and the feathery touch of barely visible snowflakes on her face. She doesn't really want to go far, she just wants the solitude, the public solitude, of the street; the un-company of passing strangers, no one embracing her, no one looking with compassion and wonder into her eyes, no one marveling at her.

She can grow tired, a little tired, of being marveled at.

She turns back at Flushing. A young man and woman walk toward her. He's white, she's black. They're in their early twenties. He's clearly one of the young artists who, like Tyler, live here because everywhere else is too expensive. He's wearing a neon-blue suit, a big black overcoat, and work boots. She (harder to identify, in terms of inclination and work) wears a tight white dress under a rabbit-fur jacket. They're laughing quietly, holding hands. As they draw nearer, Beth can see that he has a pinched and narrow face, large quizzical eyes unsettlingly answered by a paucity of jaw. She's scrawny and small-headed, showing as she laughs a set of big square teeth in a mouth that seems barely able to contain them. But they're beautiful to each other. They might be childhood friends who fell in love. They carry with them that sense of shared conspiracy, of sneaky eroticized intimacy, the joy of the forbidden, the pure giggling release of it.

As they pass Beth they say, in unison, "Happy New Year."

"Happy New Year," she replies.

They walk on, in the opposite direction.

The young couple is, it suddenly seems, what Beth came outside to see. She can't of course know what troubles may beset them, or what troubles await, but she's satisfied by the fleeting apparition of two young people who are doing fine, right now; who have each other to laugh with, to hold hands with; who can thoughtlessly pass between them the simplicity of youth, of love, of a night that must, for them, promise an endless strand of nights, a world that offers even more than they'd hoped for; that's given them this snow-blown street and the promise of home, soon, as if love and shelter were the simplest things in the world.

Beth lost her simplicity when she got her life back.

There's the burden of gratitude. She hadn't expected that. There's the feeling that, having been granted this impossible gift, she ought to do something with it. Before her diagnosis, it was enough to be in love with Tyler, to manage Liz's shop, to bake on the weekends, to make love and send e-mails and beat Barrett at Scrabble (he's never won, not once, what about *that*, Mister Yale?). There's no reason for her to do anything more, there's no rule, but now her days and nights feel too small. Something more must be expected; something more must be owed.

What, though, would it be?

She can't devote herself to a life of good works. She has a job, she and Tyler need the money. She volunteers, Saturday afternoons, at a convalescent home, reading to the old and infirm, which is satisfying but does not strike her as an adequate offering, given what she's received.

The surprise: this sense of insufficiency.

She's never told anyone about it. She's loath to admit it, even to herself.

There are times—not often, but still, there are times—when she feels ever so slightly . . . displaced, being restored to life. She had been afraid of dying but she'd been dying for quite some time, she was learning how to do it, she was getting good at it; it had become so inevitable as to feel like a home of sorts, a home*land*, an obscure but stalwart nation, ancient and reliable, untroubled; a place where the well-swept streets lead to fountained squares, where the shops and cafés are orderly and clean, where the threats of disaster and the hope of ecstatic, life-altering joy are equally out of the question.

Did Persephone sometimes find the summer sun too hot, the flowers more gaudy than beautiful? Did she ever, even briefly, think fondly of the dim silence of Hades, the cool and barren nowhere of it? Did she yearn, occasionally, for her winter release from abundance, from a world that demanded happiness of her, a world so rife with wonders that the garland and the dance were all but mandatory?

Beth reaches her building. She stands on the sidewalk, looking up. There, on the second floor, are the two living room windows, softly lit, with three Christmas lights—a red, a green, and a blue—visible, suspended from the ceiling on their thin green strand.

She stands there for longer than she'd expected to, thinking of nothing in particular, simply looking up at the windows of the place in which she lives.

A NIGHT

None of them had imagined that the canister would be hard to open. It looks like a quart-size paint can, made of brushed aluminum, but unlike a paint can, its lid is clearly meant to be screwed off. No one had suggested trying it out before they got onto the ferry.

Tyler, Barrett, and Liz huddle together at the stern, leaning against the traffic-cone-orange iron railing (the harsh orange that signals *emergency*); huddled together in part because it's windier and colder than they'd expected it to be, out in the harbor at night, even in April, but mainly because they don't want to attract the attention of the blue-uniformed crew members (are they called crew members?), who are surely not looking out to see if anyone is illegally scattering ashes off the boat, but would just as surely intervene if they caught three passengers in the act.

Tyler struggles, as unobtrusively as possible, with the intractable lid.

Spread around them is the black, light-speckled toss of the harbor, with the ferry's wake—gray-white, alive as smoke—furling out below. It is the most trafficked body of water imaginable. Barges lumber along, dark and silent, enormous, hectored by smaller boats, buzzing little lit-up toys. The ferry has just passed the turreted, slumbering silhouette of Ellis Island, and is approaching the Statue of Liberty, bright verdigris, remote, offering her little light to the charcoal-colored sky.

"Fuck," Tyler says. "Fuckity fuck fuck."

Barrett puts a calming hand on his shoulder. This is not mere inconvenience. It renders the ceremony—what there is of ceremony—comic, which is not what any of them had in mind.

Liz says, "Let me try."

She had at first declined to come, insisted it should be Tyler and Barrett alone (they couldn't possibly have brought a crowd), but Tyler and Barrett talked her into it. Liz loved Beth, Liz knew Beth before Tyler and Barrett did. And, more important, if difficult to explain—it seemed there should be a woman present.

Tyler is reluctant to give up the canister. Liz, who is particularly irritated by this particular man-fixation, reaches out impatiently. For a moment, they tussle over it, but Tyler, in the hope of remaining as uncomic as possible, lets it go.

"Mm," Liz says, twisting the lid. "Yeah, it doesn't want to unscrew, does it?"

"No," Tyler says. "It doesn't." This is not the time for any remark along the lines of, *What do you think I am, an idiot? Yeah, right, it doesn't want to unscrew.*

Liz reaches into her bag. "I have a knife," she says.

Liz would of course have a knife. She'd have the very knife she produces, a Swiss Army Knife, with a dozen different blades, a nail file, scissors, and who knows what else.

"Goddess of utility," Barrett says.

Liz extracts the nail file, slips it under the canister's lid.

"Careful," Tyler says.

At first, the nail file just scrapes ineffectively against the lid's lipless rim. Then, a little more pressure, and . . .

It releases. Liz unscrews it slightly, doesn't open it. She hands it back to Tyler.

He accepts it reluctantly. Barrett keeps his hand on his brother's shoulder.

Tyler squeezes his eyes shut, breathes heavily. He asks, "Do you think we should look inside?"

"I've seen ashes before," Liz answers. "You don't need to look inside."

Another barge rolls by, this one piled high with boxcar-size steel containers, enormous stacked boxes that couldn't possibly be painted black, but look black, from this distance. The barge is unlit. There's no sign of a pilot, or of where a pilot would be housed.

Tyler nods at the titanic black hulk, which offers no lights, which moves soundlessly, faster than the ferry. He says, "Let's wait until that thing goes by."

No one needs to comment on the world's propensity for producing these odd signs of morbidity, these memento mori, that have a way of appearing at precisely the wrong time.

They stand quietly, waiting for the black pilotless barge to pass. Manhattan blazes behind, all monolith and ziggurat. To the left, the lazy and tranquil arcs of the light-strings along the Verrazano-Narrows Bridge, answered by a modest speckling of stars.

Behind them, on the ferry: the commuters, all of whom have sensibly elected to remain in the cabin, where they sit stolidly in the green-tinged light, neither more nor less than tired wage slaves, going home.

"Okay," Barrett says, after the barge has passed. "Are we ready?"

Tyler nods. He unscrews the lid.

He does want to look inside. But he decides to obey Liz. Whatever he might see (are there bone chips, or is it merely dust; what color would the dust be?), he'd rather not see it as the contents of a can.

Is he capable of imagining that Beth's relapse is connected, somehow, to the argument they had on New Year's Eve; that he captured the attention of some terrible diety by admitting to himself that his life, freed of mortal emergency, was slightly . . . unsustaining? He is.

"I'm going to scatter some," he says. "And then I'd like each of you to, too."

Tentatively, as if he might make a wrong move (he has a momentary vision of ashes strewn across the iron-plate flooring), he lifts the canister shoulder-high, and tips it.

Nothing happens. Are they compacted? Do they need to be stirred around?

He gives the canister a small, gentle shake.

And then, a spiral of pallid brown ash flies out. It is, momentarily, a palpable stream, but it quickly catches the wind, and disperses. There are quick dull gleams of bone chips. It's a stream, then it's a modest wispy scrap of cloud, and then, an instant later, it's gone.

Tyler gives the canister to Barrett. Barrett disperses a fleeting ash-cloud of his own, hands the canister to Liz, who does the same, until nothing more emerges.

The vanishing was more complete than Tyler had expected it to be. The vastness and churn of the harbor is more intimidating than what he'd pictured, more arctic in its black and sparkling way. He hadn't been thinking of a windblown, restlessly glittering tundra, or of all these ships. He'd imagined being able to see the ashes dissolve into the water. They are, however, gone, utterly gone, dissolved in the turbulent air. The night continues. The three of them stand at the railing in silence, with yet another freighter, this one the size of a football field, passing close by, and the low moan of what Tyler can only think of as boat sound, an exhalation like that of a titanic French horn.

They'll disembark at Staten Island, then re-board the same boat back to Manhattan. The others are waiting at home. Ping and Nina and Foster and another ten or so. They've made dinner, as people do. They've agreed that no one will utter the words "celebration of life."

It seems that Tyler, Barrett, and Liz should embrace, or at least put their arms over one another's shoulders. That is not, however, what they find themselves doing. They stand close, but at slightly discreet distances. It seems, to each of them, that one of the others is about to say something unbearable, though none of them can tell whether the dreaded outpouring would be grief, or accusation, or . . . something else, something all three can imagine, but for which none of them has a name. There are, clearly, words to be said, or shouted, or hurled out over the water, but Tyler, Barrett, and Liz all believe those words to be forthcoming from one of the others. They are possessed, all of them, by an inexplicable feeling of reserve; a sense that if they aren't careful, true annihilation will descend. None of them will ever mention this to the others. Anxiously waiting, hoping for catharsis and hoping, with equal force, that they'll simply remain quiet, docile passengers, they watch the lights of Manhattan, the ice-white glow of the ferry terminal, the small bright finger of Miss Liberty, recede.

And what, exactly, are they supposed to do, now, with the empty can? None of them had thought about that.

NOVEMBER 2008

Peaple are already hauling things away, before Tyler and Barrett have brought the last of it out to the sidewalk. An elderly couple—shabbily natty, he's got licorice-black hair and has a silk scarf knotted around his neck; she's primly white-haired, in an ancient Pierre Cardin jacket, once apricot, now the color of a Band-Aid—are carrying off the two spindly chairs, one apiece. They carry the chairs seat-forward, as if prepared to offer a ride to anyone who might need one. Tyler, hefting a carton full of old DVDs, locks eyes with them as they depart, but they eschew recognition. They are deposed royalty. These chairs have been restored to them, but you can't imagine, young man, all that's been lost.

As the chair-bearing couple make their way toward Thames Street, a trio of skinny skateboard kids, each showing three inches of underwear above his jeans, zips up to examine the lighthouse-based lamp.

"It needs to be rewired," Tyler tells them, as he sets the carton full of DVDs down on the pavement.

One of the boys says, "Thanks, dude," and they're off again, as if Tyler had warned them against some hidden danger.

Barrett emerges, barely managing to carry the green Naugahyde armchair. Tyler hurries to help. When they've gotten the chair onto the sidewalk, Barrett sits down in it.

"Goodbye, old girl," he says to the chair.

"Good luck in all future endeavors."

Barrett strokes one of the chair's slick, bile-green arms. "You can get attached to just about anything, can't you?" he says.

"Some people are more sentimental than others."

"I'm not sentimental. I'm . . . compassionate."

Tyler lights a cigarette (rehab promoted him from occasional to pack-a-day smoker). They look around. The entire apartment has been arrayed on the sidewalk. Barrett has insisted on dioramas: the living room furniture is grouped together, as are the Formica-topped kitchen table and its mismatched, rickety chairs. He's done his best to reproduce the familiar disorder of Tyler and Beth's bedroom, as a curator would, with all the shabby treasures that had been gathered around the bed in more or less their former places.

Tyler is surprised by how peculiar it all looks; not only because it's out on the sidewalk but because he has, it seems, been blind to the ragtag, junky nature of their possessions. In situ, their furnishings struck him as cool, jokey, satisfyingly outré. Out here, in public, they've acquired a pathos they did not seem to possess when they were private, everyday objects. Strangers pass, browse, take something or don't. The gray sky shines down on it all, silvers the pots and pans, inspires the kitchen chairs to throw modest, formless shadows onto the sidewalk. A titanic, pewter-colored cloud rolls slowly in from the west, bringing the portent of rain to a sky that had been, until a moment ago, merely overcast. The pots and pans lose their luster, the chairs their shadows, and are rendered that much more commonplace. Just so, one might be brought before the thousand-eyed, mirror-winged god, and try warming him up with a few jokes before judgment is passed.

Barrett says, "We really don't want to keep anything? I mean, this is our last chance."

"We're keeping the TV."

"I voted to get rid of the TV."

"Then we wouldn't be able to watch the election returns."

"I think it's Obama," Barrett says. "I mean, I really think so."

Tyler shakes his tired head. "This country is so not ready for a black president. Prepare yourself for McCain. Get ready for Vice President Palin."

Barrett says, "I think this country is ready for someone who'll fix the economy and maybe, oh, stop killing about a third of the world's population."

"You're a dreamer. That's a good thing about you. If also ever so slightly annoying."

Barrett says, "I'm actually feeling a little panicky."

"You have good reason. I mean, Sarah *Palin*?"

"Actually, I meant I feel a little panicky about us getting rid of all our furniture."

"The sofa. We're keeping the sofa," Tyler says.

"That's like saying we're keeping Aunt Gertrude."

"I'm going to breathe my last breath on that sofa. Do you promise to get me onto the sofa, when the time comes?"

"If I outlive you."

"I have a feeling you will."

Barrett glances nervously around. "Don't *say* that. Do you have any idea how much you've just increased the likelihood that a cab driver is about to lose control and run me over, right here in this chair?"

"You may not be more sentimental, but you are without question more superstitious."

"I'm more amenable to the possibility of magic. How's that?"

They pause to watch a homeless man in soot-colored sweater and blackened wool pants, looking as if he's just escaped a fire, pick up the Dante vase (Korean-deli tulips, still fresh, sprout from Dante's severe and frowning head), examine it, and put it down again.

Barrett says, "Even he doesn't want that thing."

"What would he do with a vase?"

"Liz gave that to me."

"How's Liz doing?"

"Relieved, mostly. I think she was pretty much over it already."

"She hangs out sometimes. With Andrew and the new one. She's taken them to *dinner*."

"As Liz would."

"It that it? Does she do things because Liz would do them?"

"Sometimes. Don't you do things because of that?"

Tyler hesitates. "I don't think so."

"Oh, come on. Aren't there times when you don't know what to do, and you ask yourself, What would I do in a situation like this?"

"Maybe. I guess."

Tyler exhales a feather of smoke. He says, "Why didn't you didn't tell me about that goddamned light?"

"Uh, beg your pardon?"

"You told everybody else. You told Liz. You told *Andrew.*"

"This is coming up now, because . . ."

"Because it is. Because you saw the holy fucking Virgin Mother tap-dancing in the sky, and didn't say a word to me about it."

Barrett gathers himself, runs a high-speed search for reason and logic, fails to locate a vestige of either.

"That's not true. I did tell you."

"After Beth died. Which would have been, what, almost five months after you'd told every-goddamned-body else. I mean, why did you wait? No, why did you tell me at all? Why didn't you just go on forever with everybody but me knowing that this . . . *miracle* happened?"

Barrett struggles to bring himself around. Maybe it's only possible for them to have this fight in public; maybe it would feel too dangerous if strangers couldn't see and hear them. It helps, of course (does it?), that, on the sidewalk, they're surrounded by all their familiar, private things, which are for the moment neither theirs nor not theirs; that they briefly inhabit a halfway zone, between location and dispersal.

Barrett answers, "How long have you been back on drugs?"

Tyler's expression is not the one Barrett was expecting. There's nothing of the apprehended child about it. Tyler drags deeply on his cigarette, looks at Barrett in a way Barrett can only think of as provoked, as if Barrett had waited until some catastrophic interlude to accuse Tyler of neglecting a minor domestic chore.

Tyler says, "Did you think the bit about the light was going to *console* me?"

"I was afraid . . ."

Tyler waits, sucking so hard on his cigarette that the ash goes from its regular orange to fiery tangerine.

"I was afraid," Barrett continues, "it would seem like I was trying to horn in."

"English. Earth-speak."

"Like I was trying to . . . I don't know. Take over Beth's illness. Claim some sort of extra importance for myself."

"Keep going."

"Well. I suppose I supposed . . . it would seem like, Yeah, Tyler's writing a love song for her, Tyler's *marrying* her, that's all well and good, but guess what? I, Barrett, the gay little brother, have seen a *light*. In the *sky*."

"So you didn't want to tell me about the most amazing thing that's ever happened to you because you were afraid you might make the wrong impression."

"I started to wonder . . ."

"Uh-huh."

"I started to wonder if I really *had* seen anything, or if I'd just . . . made it up."

"And why would you make something like that up?" Tyler flings his cigarette away, lights another.

"Uh, like, maybe to feel like *somebody*? I wasn't doing anything to help Beth get better . . ."

"Nobody was, nobody could . . ."

"I couldn't write a song for her, I couldn't marry her."

"So you cooked yourself up a hallucination."

Barrett says, "I didn't know. It seemed so undeniable, at first. But over time, I started wondering. I kept waiting for, I don't know. Vision number two."

"You think they come in pairs?"

"I think I've been trying too hard for too long."

"Come again?"

"I've given up the need to be important. Trying to matter. In that mover-and-shaker kind of way."

"I can't say I've observed a lot of moving," Tyler says. "Or shaking, come to think of it."

"But there's a difference between not pursuing worldly ambitions and no longer feeling like a failure for not pursuing them. I've been wondering if that's what the light meant. Like, you're watched, you're accounted for, you don't have to be important, you don't have to have your picture in a magazine."

"Didn't we just decide the light was some kind of mirage?"

"That's the thing," Barrett says. "It doesn't matter if it was real, or if I just imagined it. It adds up, either way."

Tyler's face changes in a way it never has before. His face resembles their mother's. Has he known, all these years, how to summon her joke's-on-you smile, her cynical arch of brow? Has he been saving this trick for a crucial moment?

Tyler says, "You want something of your own, don't you?"

Barrett can't seem to answer that.

"You want something that has nothing to do with me," Tyler says. "Am I right?"

Barrett says, "I want to make sure about something. You think we're going to kind of barrel-jump over you doing coke in secret. Right?"

"I'm not," Tyler answers.

"I found a coke vial in your nightstand drawer."

"*Old* one. I'd *forgotten* about it. How many times have we talked about this?"

"But, really?"

"This is like some kind of Asian justice system, isn't it? Like, once you've been proven guilty, you can never be not guilty again."

"You think that's how Asian justice systems work?"

"I have no idea. I guess it's racist, huh?"

Tyler sits down on the chair beside Barrett's, the innocent-looking but fiendishly uncomfortable wing-back chair, upholstered in faded red silk, which Barrett has placed, in relation to the green Naugahyde, exactly where it stood in the apartment.

Barrett says, "I've started going to church again."

"Have you?"

"Having a crisis about God after Beth died seemed too . . . lame, I guess."

"How's that working for you? Church, I mean."

"I couldn't say, exactly. I just go."

"But nothing happens?" Tyler says.

"I wouldn't say nothing."

"You don't pray. You don't sing the hymns."

"No. I sit in a pew at the back."

"You must *feel* something."

"Peaceful. Semi-peaceful. That's about it."

This is not, Tyler decides, the time or place for a detailed metaphysical discussion. He says, "I'm going to go over and check out the new place."

"I'll come by after work. Okay if I bring Sam along?"

"Sure."

"Really sure?"

"What exactly is this thing of yours about me not liking Sam?" Tyler pulls another cigarette from his pack, fumbles in his jeans pocket for his lighter.

"Uh, because he's coming between us?"

"Beth didn't come between us."

Barrett says, "I was married to Beth too."

Tyler tries to light his cigarette with a pack of Life Savers, puts the Life Savers back into his pocket, finds the actual lighter.

"Then I can be married to Sam, along with you, right?" he says. He lights his cigarette, takes a deep drag. Here, once again, is that delicious, slightly noxious flow into his lungs, the sour-sweetness of it. As he exhales, he watches the smoke disappear.

"I don't think so. I can't see it. I'm sorry."

Tyler takes another drag, watches the smokestream.

Barrett says, "I'm kind of excited about getting all new furniture."

"I am too."

"You're sure about this? We can still reclaim some of it. Oh, look, there goes the kitchen table."

A young couple, tattooed and spike-haired, is carrying off the kitchen table. The boy cries, over his shoulder, "Thanks, guys."

Tyler offers a jaunty wave of acknowledgment. He says to Barrett, "I'm exactly haunted enough, without the furniture."

Both watch the kitchen table make its way west. Barrett sings the opening phrase of the theme song from *The Jeffersons*. "*We're movin' on up . . .*"

"That's all I can remember," he adds.

Tyler says, "From a total shithole to a semi-shithole."

The kitchen table, borne by its new owners, turns the corner and is gone.

"I've been thinking about an old French farm table," Barrett says. "You know the kind I mean? They're about a hundred years old. They're really long, and they have these great nicks and scars on them."

"Remember, we're still on a budget."

"I know. But, hey, we've got a hit album . . ."

"We've got a not-quite-finished album that'll probably sell about three dozen copies."

Barrett says, "You know, if you're hopeful, if you're even a little bit happy about something that might happen, it doesn't affect the outcome. You could still give yourself a period of optimism, even if it all falls apart. This, coming from the superstitious one."

Tyler doesn't reply. He tosses his half-smoked cigarette to the pavement, crushes it out with his boot-heel. He gets up, for the last time, from the world's least user-friendly chair.

"I guess that's all of it," he says.

"I think so," Barrett answers. "I'll go back upstairs in a minute, and check."

"So. I'll see you later. At our *new home*."

"See you later."

Tyler does not, however, leave; not right away. A sense of what could only be called awkwardness sets in.

"This is strange," Tyler says.

"Moving is always strange, right?"

"Yes. Absolutely."

They do the eye thing. They pass the recognition back and forth.

Still, there's a sense of leave-taking; a remote hint—a whisper, barely—of farewell. Which is silly. Right? They'll see each other tonight. In their new home.

"Later," Tyler says. He heads down Knickbocker, to Morgan.

Barrett lingers awhile. He's not eager to relinquish the strange pleasure of sitting in the green chair, surrounded by the ever-diminishing offerings that had, just yesterday, been daily articles, watching the apartment disappear, piece by piece. There goes the hula-girl lamp, in the arms of a henna-haired girl. Surprising it lasted as long as it did. Barrett briefly imagines himself remaining in the chair until everything else is gone and it's just him, alone, sitting in front of the mustard-colored, aluminum-clad building like a deposed Russian aristocrat, contemplating with wonder his new life as an ordinary, unprivileged citizen. The dacha has fallen into deep decline. Its interior dampness resists the effects of every stove and fireplace; the damask that remains on its walls is mere scraps of faded scarlet; the ceilings sag and the servants have grown so decrepit they no longer provide help, but need help themselves. Still, life has been lived there, and the future, even if it reveals itself as improvement, smells of incipient snow, and the stodgy, steely scent of windswept railway platforms.

T yler calls Liz on his way to the L. She answers. Now that she's single again, she answers her phone sometimes. She'd been one of those people who always let calls go to voice mail.

Does this imply some nameless anticipation, a wished-for intercession of chance or fortune? Tyler hopes not.

"Hey," he says.

"Are you all moved out?" she asks.

"Every stick of it. Well, Barrett's doing the final check. I'm on my way to the new place."

He strides along Morgan Street. Goodbye, chain-link fence topped with razor wire. Goodbye, old lady's window, with the glass squirrel family frozen forever in mid-cavort on the windowsill.

"Is it strange?" Liz asks.

"A little. It's strange to be doing it without Beth."

"That's what I meant."

"She didn't hate Bushwick, though. I mean, there's that."

"She was funny that way. She didn't really hate it any-where."

Tyler says, "Do you think you could meet me at the new place?"

"I have to open the store in forty-five minutes."

"Barrett can open."

"Do you want me to come?"

"Kind of. I don't really exactly feel like walking in there alone."

"I'll come, then."

"Thank you."

"I can be there in about twenty-five minutes."

"Thank you," Tyler says again.

.

Tyler waits for Liz on the stoop of the new building, smok-ing a cigarette. Hello, Avenue C. Hello, new café next door to a skeevy deli, shelves half stocked, that's got to be a front for drug dealing. Hello, red-jacketed young buck, nice faux-hawk, good luck getting around the three ancient women trading complaints in a foreign language (Polish, Ukrainian?), who've spread themselves across the sidewalk, a human block-ade, all carrying plastic bags from Key Food, moving at the pace of a Labor Day parade.

When Liz turns the corner, at the far end of the block, Tyler experiences a moment of non-recognition, sees Liz as he'd see her if she were just another stranger, turning off Ninth Street onto Avenue C.

Briefly he sees a tall, serious woman, something of the ranch hand about her—the booted stride, the squared shoulders. Liz walks like a man. There's the chocolate-colored leather jacket as well, and the gray hair pulled carelessly back. She's been called in to break that bronco, the one no one else can ride . . .

And then she's Liz again.

"Hello," Tyler says. He throws his cigarette to the curb, stands up. They embrace quickly, semi-formally, as if a gesture of cheerful courage is required. Tyler thinks of mourners, at a wake.

"Have you been waiting long?" she asks.

"Naw. A few minutes. Checking out the new nabe."

"And?"

"More people. Fewer of them desperate and insane."

"The desperate and insane are everywhere. You've only been here a few minutes."

Tyler holds open the door for her, and they walk into the lobby. It's arid and crepuscular, semi-lit by a flickering fluorescent circle. It smells of ammonia and, more faintly, of wood smoke.

It is, however, a notable improvement over the pasty yellow, violently bright vestibule in Bushwick.

They take the elevator (there's an elevator!) to the fourth floor. Tyler tries his new key in the lock of the door marked 4B. It works. The door sighs open, a sound of exhausted yet unremitting patience.

Tyler and Liz stand in the small foyer.

"This is so much better," she says.

"Hard to deny." He steps loudly (his boots seem to make

an unnatural clatter in this shadowy silence) across the coffee-colored floorboards, into the living room. Liz follows.

The living room is empty, in more than the literal way. Whoever lived here previously left no traces, not even ghostly ones. The place in Bushwick had had such history of inhabitation; it had been so assiduously "improved" by generations of tenants. This apartment has, it seems, merely aged, its walls a dingy pancake-batter color that was once white, dotted here and there with a nail hole where a picture hung. Its dark floorboards are scratched in places, but appear to have remained essentially unaltered over the course of eighty years or more. No one has stripped or painted them, no one has covered them in varnish.

In the middle of the room, like a proud and silent queen, stands the sofa, delivered yesterday by Two Guys with a Van.

"There she is," Liz says.

"I've told Barrett I want to die on this couch. Remind him, okay?"

Tyler sits on the sofa. He is, briefly, like a dog, returning gratefully to its bed, its basket, piled with hair-specked blankets, in a corner of the kitchen.

"Have you decided about paint yet?" Liz asks.

"Barrett's still holding out for all white."

"You can compromise."

"He's being funny about this. It's like, if there's a single wall in the whole place that isn't white, he won't be able to sleep at night."

Liz takes off her jacket, drops it onto the floor (there's nowhere else to put it), comes and sits beside Tyler on the sofa.

"And so," Tyler says. "We live here, now." He sings the snatch of *The Jeffersons'* theme song. "*We're movin' on up . . .*"

"How's the new song coming?" she asks.

"Okay. No. I don't know. It feels . . . salvageable. Maybe."

Liz leans forward, gives him a long and penetrating look.

"It's good, what's happening," she says.

"I know. I know that."

"And I know it's weird."

"I'm sorry she didn't get to see me have a little bit of success."

"She knew you'd be successful, eventually."

"You know the really nutty thing about Beth? She didn't care about that."

"Not for herself. For you."

"Yeah. Well. True. Let's say I'd like for her to see me be happier, then. I'd like to *be* happier."

"You will be," Liz says.

"I used to write those songs for Beth."

"I know."

"Now I'm just writing them . . . because, hey, what else am I going to do?"

And then, to his surprise, Tyler can't seem to catch his breath. He leans forward, plants his elbows on his knees, sucks at the unyielding air.

"Are you okay?" Liz asks.

It is, it seems, difficult for Tyler to speak. Liz waits. She has the good sense to wait. Tyler pulls in a draught of oxygen, which doesn't quite fill his lungs but will do, it'll have to do, it's the best he can manage.

He finds that he's able to say, "I just . . . It's just that . . . Beth died. And my music got better."

"Your music got a wider audience. After you've been at it for years."

"No, it got better. And therefore" (breathe, breathe) "reached a wider audience."

"Well. I suppose, when you've gone through something like that . . ."

Tyler struggles, again, for breath. Panic attack, he says to himself. This is a panic attack.

Breathe. Do your best.

Liz says, "It's not like you made a deal with the devil."

Tyler manages another breath. A three-quarters breath. His head is tingling dizzily.

"No," he says. "I didn't."

Liz strokes his shoulder with the flat of her hand, as if she were calming a horse.

"The thing is," Tyler manages to say. "The thing is. If I'd been offered a deal like that. I think I might have taken it."

"No. You wouldn't have."

"What I mean is. I think I might have cared more about writing that song for Beth than I did about Beth herself."

"That's not true."

"It might be. It might be true."

Liz nods. She is, without question, the only person Tyler knows who could let an assertion like that pass unremarked, not because she doesn't believe it, but because she knows the story of human desire, in all its squeamish particulars.

Tyler finally catches a breath. It's like a sail, filling with wind. The world is flying away, he's no one he recognizes. His song—his lament, his long howl, his first work with synthesizers because he didn't trust his own voice, his voice was suddenly too personal—that song, with the slowed-down, full-octave-deeper voice, a voice that resembles Tyler's in the general, DNA-pool way of second cousins; that

Captain Ahab voice, cold and obsessed and—what did that blogger say?—calmly and rationally deranged—got just fewer than three hundred thousand hits on YouTube (YouTube was Barrett's idea), and, after the second posted song (even more sonorous, more operatically inconsolable—had it been his attempt to undo the implausible success of the first?) got almost four hundred thousand hits and was touted by a flotilla of bloggers (who *are* those people?), landed him a deal, a mini-deal, granted, but with one of the truly no-bullshit indies, which means enough money up front to rent this better apartment; which means the possibility of a future, a life that's no longer invisible. Obscure (probably) but not wholly invisible (he's surprised by the difference between "obscure" and "invisible"). He's finally attained obscurity. Beth's ashes have been swallowed by the harbor and yes, he adored her, and yes, he feels as well a terrible, unspeakable freedom without her; without his desire to console her, to offer her something worth having, to move her and please her, the girl who rolled out crusts and collected playing cards she found on the street (claiming it was her lifelong ambition to assemble a full deck); the girl who was glad to be just about anywhere; who asked for, and possessed, so little.

They argued, on New Year's Eve. They didn't make love, after Beth came back from her walk. And then, less than a week later, the symptoms came rampaging back.

Tyler looks imploringly at Liz. His eyes are wet, his breath still iffy.

He moves in on her. It happens more quickly than usual; there's no gesture of seduction, however brief. He is at one moment looking into her face, helpless and imploring, and, at the next, he's pressing his lips to hers, as if her mouth were an oxygen mask. She holds the kiss, returns it, neither hungry nor maidenly. Her lips are pliant but forceful, there's *will* behind her kiss, she's not desperate but she's not accommodating. Her mouth is clean in an herbal way, no herb in particular but that sense of green rampancy. Tyler presses himself to her, pushes her down onto her back. He can breathe now, it seems. He can breathe again. He takes one of her breasts in his hand, first over her shirt, then under it. He unbuttons her shirt, cups one of her breasts. It fits entirely within his hand. Liz's breasts are so small they haven't sagged, there's nothing *to* sag. With Tyler's touch, her nipple (biggish for her tiny breasts, raspberry-colored) stiffens. She makes a sound that's more sigh than moan. She buries her hands in his hair.

Tyler gets up onto his knees, pulls his jeans and boxers down. His hard-on pops. Liz kicks off her boots, pulls her own jeans and thong off, shimmies them down to her ankles and thrashes them away, spreads her legs around Tyler's hips. Tyler gets only the briefest look at her crotch—the trimmed line of her dark pubic hair, the robust pink of her labia—before pushing back down onto her.

They both know they have to do this quickly. He slides his dick into her. She sighs more loudly, but it's still a sigh, not a sex moan, though this time there's a soft gasp at the end. Tyler is inside her, here's the heat, the powerful wet hold, and fuck, he's about to come already. He holds off, lets his cock rest in her, lies on top, his face pressed to her cheek (he can't seem to look directly at her), until she says, "Don't wait."

"Are you sure?"

"I'm sure."

He thrusts once, cautiously. He thrusts again, and he's

gone, he's off into the careening nowhere. He lives for seconds in that soaring agonizing perfection. It's this, only this, he's lost to himself, he's no one, he's obliterated, there's no Tyler at all, there's only . . . He hears himself gasp in wonder. He falls into an ecstatic burning harmedness, losing, lost, unmade.

And is finished.

He nestles his head against her neck. She kisses him, chastely, on the temple, then makes it clear that she wants to be released. He doesn't argue. He rolls off her, wedges himself against the back of the sofa.

She stands, gets quickly into her thong and jeans, bends to put her boots back on. Neither of them speaks. Liz picks up her jacket from the floor, shrugs into it. Tyler remains lying on the sofa, regarding her with an expression of cowed and wondering helplessness. When she's fully dressed she stands over him, strums her fingertips across his face, and leaves the apartment. Tyler hears her close the door softly behind herself, hears the muffled thump of her boots as she descends the stairs.

The girl has been deciding about a necklace for almost half an hour. She leans over the modest glass-topped jewelry case, attentive as a surgeon.

While she's been deciding, two women have bought a pair of studded black Converse high-tops and a vintage Courtney Love T-shirt (which Barrett will miss). A teenage boy has been denied, by his mother, one of the airbrushed skateboards. A man (not young) in cut-off shorts and a bomber jacket has expressed his bemused outrage over the fact that the sunglasses start at two hundred dollars.

Barrett leaves the girl alone with her decision about the necklace. They don't hover, in Liz's shop. Liz is firm about that. You greet people when they come in, assure them that you'll help them if they need help, and, after that, you leave them alone. If they try on clothes and ask how they look, you are polite but truthful. No one leaves the shop with a pair of jeans that are unflatteringly tight around an ass that doesn't merit that degree of scrutiny, no one leaves in a T-shirt that emphasizes a sallow complexion. People will either buy something or they won't. Wynne, who's taken over Beth's job, had to be encouraged, when she started, to be less helpful with the customers.

At the moment it's just Barrett and the necklace-examining girl. Barrett is folding T-shirts. A surprise about retail: it's essentially an ongoing act of folding, and re-folding, and re-re-folding, interrupted by the greeting of customers, and periodic transactions. Barrett has discovered in it a certain Zen calm, and even a pride of expertise. He can fold a T-shirt into a perfect square, every time, in less than ten seconds.

The girl says, "Sorry for taking so long."

"Take all the time you need," Barrett answers.

She says, "Could you come here and take a look?"

"Of course."

Barrett tucks another precisely folded T-shirt onto its shelf. The girl, early twenties, is tall and frail-looking, not sickly but possessed of a pale, hesitant aspect. Her dark red hair hangs loosely, just below her shoulder blades. Her face, scattered with pinpoint freckles, has the small-featured, reverent aspect of a Fra Angelico angel. She was, Barrett thinks, ignored when she was younger—one of the girls who is neither tortured nor sought after—and she's still unaccustomed to the attention paid her by an adult world more amenable to beauty in its less usual forms.

Barrett steps behind the jewelry counter. The girl has placed, carefully, two necklaces onto the black velvet square Barrett set out for her when she came into the shop.

"I've gotten it down to two," she says.

Arrayed on the velvet are one of the fetish necklaces—a silver Buddha, a tourmaline, a tiny gold horseshoe—and a strand of black silk cord, from which hangs an uncut diamond, slightly larger than a pea, with its dim, ice-gray shine.

"I know it won't help if I tell you they're both beautiful," Barrett says.

She laughs, then stops suddenly, as if Barrett might take laughter as an insult.

"I'm being ridiculous," she says. "It's just a necklace."

"No, you're going to wear it, you should feel sure."

She nods abstractedly, scrutinizing the necklaces.

Barrett says, "If you pick one and it doesn't feel right, you can come back and exchange it for the other."

She nods again. She says, "I'm getting married."

She looks up at him. Her eyes darken slightly, take on moister depths.

Barrett asks, "Are you looking for a necklace to wear to your wedding?"

"Oh, no. The wedding. I mean, it'll be a white dress, and his mother's pearls."

She pauses. "His family is Italian," she adds.

She's unsure, then, about what will happen when she permits the man's family to claim her, as if she were a shy village girl with a modest dowry, married to the son of an embattled ruling family as part of an uneasy truce. She imagines herself at clattering, cantankerous dinners, where the boys throw scraps to the mastiffs and the mother expresses, by way of pointed glances, her doubts about the heartiness of the heirs to come.

The girl wants to walk out of the shop as the girl wearing this necklace—this talisman, this assertion. *I chose this on my own, it has nothing to do with my fiancé.* It is, in its small way, a distillation of her separateness, of a privacy that can't be violated.

Barrett says, "Okay. I'm going to close my eyes, and point to one. See if you feel happy about the one I point to, or disappointed that I didn't point to the other one."

She smiles shyly. "All right," she says.

Barrett shuts his eyes, points. He's chosen the necklace with the three fetishes.

"Oh," the girl says.

"You want the other one."

"Yes, I think I do."

"There you have it, then."

She carefully lifts from the velvet the silk cord with the icy, asymmetrical little diamond. She drapes it around her neck, has a moment's trouble with the clasp, gets it.

"It's good," Barrett says. "It looks right."

The girl turns to the small oval mirror on top of the jewelry case. She seems happy about what she sees.

"It's beautiful," she says.

Barrett is poised to say, Don't marry that guy. You love him right now, he probably dazzles you in bed, but you know, in a way you can't articulate, not even to yourself, that you're about to be usurped, you're about to go live in a world where you won't be welcome, and you don't have enough history yet as a pretty girl, you're still too grateful for his attentions. Gratitude will fade and you'll still be going to those Sunday dinners in Jersey, where you'll be merely tolerated, until he begins to side with his family, to regret the rebelliousness of his choice, to wonder why he married you and not the wisecracking big-breasted Italian girl his mother had in mind for him. He's a citizen of his mother, he probably does love you now, but his interest will fade, he'll start compiling a list of your lacks, he'll get sullen and resentful over crimes you don't know you've committed.

What Barrett says is, "Yeah, it's beautiful. Are you set, then?"

"Yes. Finally. Thank you for being so patient."

"These are serious choices. In their way, I mean. So. Cash or credit card?"

She produces a MasterCard from a slim green wallet. He runs the card, she signs the slip.

"Would you like it in a box?" he asks.

"No. Thank you. I'm going to wear it."

"Good luck," he says.

She gives him a questioning look.

"It's wedding etiquette," Barrett tells her. "You congratulate the groom, and wish the bride good luck."

"I didn't know that."

A pause arrives. For a moment, it seems as if Barrett and the woman are the ones getting married.

"Thank you," she says, and walks out of the shop. Barrett returns to the folding of T-shirts.

·

Liz arrives almost an hour later. Her face is unlike itself, though Barrett can't interpret this unfamiliar version of her, this expression he's never seen before. He can only think of it as calmly appalled.

"Everything okay here?" she says.

"Fine," he answers.

Liz takes off her jacket, goes and hangs it on the hook in the storage room. She returns and stands straight-backed behind the counter, checking the register, the way a spinster who runs a boardinghouse might count the spoons after supper has been served.

"Everything okay with *you*?" Barrett asks.

She pauses, considering.

"I was just at the apartment. With Tyler," she says.

Barrett goes and straightens the skateboards that hang on the wall at the back. Liz says, "I think we're not going to reorder the skateboards."

"I like the skateboards. They kind of sell. Sometimes."

"They're just starting to feel a little . . . contrived," Liz says. "Like we're trying too hard to be cool."

"Got it."

"The thing about Tyler is, I couldn't seem to talk to him, or just hold him, the way most people would have."

"You were there. I'm sure that was all he needed."

"I never wanted to be one of those women," Liz says.

"Come again?"

"I mean, one of those women who are, you know, consoling and maternal and all."

"You're not that kind of woman. Which is one of the reasons one loves you."

She says, "I beat my father up when I was fifteen."

"Really?"

"He was violent. I've never told you about this, right?"

"No, you don't talk about your family much. Well, you finally told me about your sister, but it had to be New Year's Eve, there had to be drugs, and miracles . . ."

"He wasn't take-out-an-order-of-protection violent," she says. "Just regular violent, he'd get mad and he'd cuff us, with the back of his hand, all three of us, my mother and my sister and me."

A silence passes.

Presently, Liz says, "For a long time it just seemed like, I don't know, part of our lives. Part of what happens. But one night, my sister got home late. She would have been thirteen then. She was dating a junior. Which was a big thing for her. She was this shy, pretty little girl, and to her total amazement she started ninth grade and was suddenly seeing this insanely hot guy. So she got home a little late one night, and our father started in on her about that, then he started accusing her of having sex with the boy. This, as our father put it, thug."

"Was she? Having sex with the guy?"

"Of course she was. She told our father no, though. But he hit her anyway."

"Oh."

"It was just the regular thing that happened. But that night, I don't know. My sister was so happy, she wasn't doing anything wrong, she was in love for the first time, and I couldn't stand seeing her get punished for it."

"Maybe thirteen is a little young to be having sex," Barrett says. He hurriedly adds, "Not that anybody should get knocked around for it."

"That boy she was seeing, I don't remember his name, it didn't last all that long, him and my sister, and years later he died, he was in a train crash in Europe . . ."

"Stay with the story, okay?"

"Well. I picked up one of those little shovel things by the fireplace, you know, the things you use to scoop out ashes. I hardly even thought about it. I picked it up and hit him with it. Our father. On the side of his head."

"*Go*, girl. Um, was that inappropriate?"

"I didn't hit him all that hard. I mean, I'd never done anything like that. I was scrappy, I got into fights at school, but they were just girl fights. I'd never picked something up and hit somebody with it. I didn't really know how to do it. So I kind of clipped him. As opposed to hitting him."

"And . . ."

"He turned and stared at me. In complete astonishment. Like, the aliens have landed. And I thought, Oh, I've really started something, haven't I?"

"And so you . . ."

"I hit him again. Really hard, this time. Right across the face."

"No shit."

"He went down. Not *down* down, he just sort of crumpled to his knees. I stood over him with that shovel thing in my hands. And I said to him, 'If you ever hit any of us again, I'll kill you.' I said that."

"And he . . ."

"It was the strangest thing. I was just a fifteen-year-old girl with this tiny weapon, he could have jumped me so easily, he could have murdered me. But he didn't. He didn't even get up. He stayed on his knees on the floor. And he gave me this awful look. It was so not what I was expecting. It was, well, a look of defeat. Like, all I'd had to do, all any of us had had to do, was tell him to stop."

"Oh."

"It was sort of . . . amazing. Neither of us knew what to do next. I started feeling ridiculous. Standing there with that little shovel in my hands. I didn't feel heroic. Then, after a while, he stood up and left the room. He went upstairs. He went into his and Mom's bedroom, shut the door, and that was that. He showed up for breakfast the next morning as if nothing had happened."

"And after that?"

"He never hit any of us again. Plus, this is strange, after that it was like he was a little bit afraid of me, and also maybe loved me a little more than he had before. But, you know, ever since then, I've felt like, No man is ever going to fuck with me. I'm sure I'd felt that way for a long time already, I just kind of think of myself as having turned into . . . *myself*, the night I hit my father with that stupid little shovel."

Barrett can't shed the conviction that he should say something, nor can he think of anything to say.

"Here's a funny thing," Liz says. "My sister was a little bit afraid of me after that, too. I thought I'd rescued her. I had rescued her, in a way. But it didn't really bring us closer. It seems to have meant I was dangerous in ways she'd never thought I could be."

"Why exactly are you thinking about all this now?"

"Now my sister is schizophrenic and she's on drugs that make her slow and fat, she's living with our parents again . . ."

"Why are you thinking about this *now*?"

"Because," Liz says. "I suppose because today there was this moment, with Tyler, that, well, reminded me of that night. With my father."

"You didn't hit Tyler."

"I don't think I've ever really been in love," Liz says.

"Never?"

"Oh, I've loved all kinds of guys. Some more than others. But there's this other thing I hear people talk about, Beth used to talk about it, that I've never really *recognized*. It's sort of this feeling of abandonment, of . . . I'm not sure how to put this . . . of crossing over, inhabiting another person and letting him inhabit you. I'm not putting this very well . . ."

"No, it's okay, I understand."

"I've never felt that. I never really exactly missed it. Until. This is funny. Until just now. I wanted to feel it with Tyler."

"Tyler's not your lover."

"I just couldn't seem to comfort him. And I wanted to. For him. And for Beth. I suppose I wanted to do what Beth would have done."

"Beth was a different kind of person," Barrett says.

"Of course she was. But it's not like doing whatever you can to make another person feel better is such a huge talent. Most people can do it."

"Tyler loves you. Tyler respects you. You probably did him more good just now than you can imagine."

"You know what? I'm not really thinking about Tyler right now. I'm thinking about myself. I'm thinking about this perfectly simple human thing I can't seem to do."

"You can do a lot of other things."

Liz looks through the receipts again.

She says, "I had the strangest idea, as I was coming to the shop. I started thinking, wondering, I started wondering. I've always thought I won with my father. I stopped him from hitting us. And on my way here, right there on the L train, I started wondering if he won, after all. If he won by making me hit him."

Both are quiet for a while. Barrett offers silent thanks to all the customers who don't come in.

Liz says, finally, "Do you really think the skateboards don't seem slightly desperate?"

"I do. Maybe we should balance them out with something a little more sophisticated. What would you think about some really high-end leather jackets? New ones, not just the vintage."

"Do you think you could take care of the shop, if I went away for a while?" she says.

"Where would you go?"

"I don't know. I feel like I'd like to go somewhere else. For a while."

"This is a little sudden, don't you think?"

"Have you heard from Andrew lately?" she asks.

"He called me. He wants to meet me in Central Park tonight, for some reason."

"That's nice."

"It's more like, peculiar. I mean, why me?"

"He likes you," she says.

"Doesn't he more or less like everybody?"

"Maybe it's because you like him. No one else did."

"People just thought he was . . . Not right. For you."

"Is he still with Stella?"

"Uh-huh."

"Don't look at me like that, it's good, she's good. For him."

Barrett says, "She's a little . . ."

"She's not the sharpest tack in the box. I know. She's a weaver, did you know that?"

"Oh, well, she's just kind of a funny girl, really. It seems that she's a yoga teacher and, yeah, some sort of weaver, I mean, she's actually got a loom . . ."

"She's okay, though," Liz says.

"She is. You want to hear something funny? The last time I saw them, she told me she was psychic."

"She adores Andrew, though. Somebody should adore Andrew."

"Why did you stay with him all that time? I never quite got around to asking you. I guess it seemed rude. Or something."

"Oh, you know," she says. "Having him around sort of . . . took care of things. He was sexy and a little dull and he never caused any trouble and so there was one less thing I had to think about."

"Not the worst of all possible arrangements."

"I don't think I'm going to get another one."

"Uh, another what?"

"Another sexy silly boy who sticks around until he comes to his senses and goes off with a girl his own age. I think I'm done with that."

"Probably just as well."

"Are you in love with Sam?" she asks.

"Oh. I don't know. It's only been a few months . . ."

"You know. Or so rumor has it. I hear you know pretty quickly."

Barrett says, "He's not anything like who I was expecting."

Liz nods, as if receiving a bit of news—neither good nor bad—that's been long anticipated.

"I've been thinking," she says, "that I might want to go west for a while. California, maybe."

"California is great."

"I might go. I'm thinking about it."

"I could take care of the shop, if you want me to."

"You're better at it than I am, by now."

"Not true."

"You're a nicer person. You pay attention to the customers. You care about them. I just hope they'll buy something, without me having to bullshit them into it."

"What do you think you'd do in California?" Barrett asks.

"I don't know. Right now, I stop at the idea of going there. It's a blank, beyond that."

Barrett asks, "Do you ever think about that light?"

"What light?"

"The one we saw. Up in the sky."

"Not really. Do you?"

Barrett nods, sadly. "All the time," he says.

"But you haven't seen it again?"

"No. I haven't."

"Honey. I was stoned. You were . . . oh, well, who knows what you were. You'd just been dumped by asshole number seventeen, why wouldn't you want an airplane behind a cloud to be something more?"

"And then Beth got better . . ."

Liz looks at him with compassionate steadiness.

"And then she died."

"I know. But she had those months, didn't she?"

"I just don't think a light in the sky had anything to do with it."

Barrett says, "I keep waiting for . . . something."

"What would that be?"

"Another sign, I guess. A follow-up."

"A sign of . . ."

"Like, there's something more than just us. You know, more than looking for love and wondering where to go for dinner and selling necklaces to some poor girl who's about to marry the wrong guy . . ."

Liz says, "Everybody wants that to be true."

"And what if it is?"

"Right," she says. "What if it is?"

She says it in a tone of patient, slightly vexed consolation. Sure, sweetheart, what if that flea market painting turns out to be an unknown Winslow Homer, what if the number you've been playing all these years finally, this time, wins the lottery?

A moment later, a couple walks into the shop, two young men with post-punk haircuts. One says to the other, "Sparkle, Neely, sparkle."

Liz says hello to them.

"Hi there," one says, and the other laughs, as if his boyfriend has made a joke.

"Let us know if we can help with anything," Liz says.

"We will."

The young men start browsing. Liz goes through the receipts again. Barrett goes back to folding T-shirts, although he's folded all of them already.

It's almost three o'clock, which means Liz left the apartment more than four hours ago. Tyler has been lying on the sofa ever since, in his nimbus of floating glow, contemplating Liz and music.

That thing with Liz . . . Hm. That thing with Liz . . .

How long have they been having sex? Since Beth's diagnosis? Longer than that? Strange of them, to have been secretive about it; they who keep almost no secrets at all, not really for moral purposes but because the truth is so much easier, the truth is right there, no efforts at modification or embellishment required.

When did they stop? It must have been when Beth recovered, though Tyler has the sense—more dimly recollected dream than memory—that it went on longer than that. He seems to remember not so much the sex as the shame; the conviction that he and Liz were, toward the end of it, committing a shameful act. Although he did, no denying it, flirt with shame all the while.

He'd been so lonely and panicked, as Beth diminished. Liz was there. Liz was as unsentimental as it's possible for anyone to be.

Tyler prefers, he's preferred all along, not to seriously entertain (not at length, not in depth) the possibility that, for Liz, the attraction has always resided in his ever-so-slightly skanky middle-agedness; that he is, for her, the un-Andrew—no blank-faced young Olympian, no visitation from a parallel dimension of hormone-gloried youth, no Ariel who'll soon be off to perform other enchantments; just a regular Joe, Mister Easy, Mister Grateful.

He and Liz not only never spoke about it to anyone, they never spoke about it to each other. It was something they did, but it was not a topic, ever.

He didn't even tell Barrett.

The funny thing: it's Barrett, most likely, who'd have minded. Barrett who'd have felt shut out. Barrett is after all the one who considers himself deposed; who was, it seems (to Barrett), at one moment the hero of the story, crackling with possibility, bastard child of Hamlet and Oscar Wilde; Barrett who walked the high school halls trailing his invisible cloak of silver lamé chain mail, graciously ascending to realms beyond his older brother's spliffs and folk guitar, his football-team regularhood; Barrett who, at the next moment (or so it seems, to Barrett), was searching the sofa cushions for lost coins, asking himself whether those leftovers were still safe to eat, wondering if love might arrive on the next train, or the next, alert to the whistle of its approach.

Beth wouldn't have minded that Tyler was fucking her best friend. She'd have known exactly what it did and did not mean.

And here, unbidden . . . worse than unbidden, fucking *revealing* . . . is a renegade memory, sharp and strange as snow falling into the bedroom . . .

His mother (his and Barrett's, do try to remember that) is perched in the bleachers, front row, wearing eccentric eyeglasses and an elaborate scarf. Their father must be off getting Cokes, or the lap robe she'd insisted she didn't need. Tyler, having made the game's first first down (by inches, but still), knows he has to go and stand before her (his triumphs are rare), offering the gladiator's lowered sword, the matador's severed bull's-ear. He is helmeted and padded, costumed, potently impersonal, with black grease streaks under his eyes.

"Hey, Mom."

He likes, he momentarily likes, his unrecognizability, in football gear—thus armored, he could be any woman's son. He has *chosen* this mother: her enormous hoop earrings, her cropped black cap of hair, the powerful magnolia waft of her *eau de whatever*. He feels as if he's committing not a filial duty, but an act of gallantry.

She, of course, is costumed too. Tyler's job is to resemble. Hers is to (as she herself would say) "Put her best foot forward."

She looks down the bleachers, ten feet above Tyler's upturned face (so little of it revealed: eyes dimmed to pond water by the black grease swatches, modest jut of nose over the guard behind which his mouth is concealed). She wraps her cashmere-sleeved arms coquettishly around the dull gray of the railing (does she know how obvious she is, how posed and *done up*, I mean the whole Countess von Hoopendorf thing, she must know, she's too smart not to, she must have some hidden purpose . . .). She leans forward and down, putting her face (grainy with the powder that shows lividly in the stadium lights, the dark pink, just-been-slapped shade she uses), and says, "Nice play."

"Thanks."

She looks around stagily, an amateur actress in a second-rate play, searching with elaborate hopefulness for someone the audience knows to be lost, or vanished, or dead. She says (she must speak loudly, to be heard at all), "Where's your brother tonight?"

For emphasis, she looks again, searching the crowd, as if she expected to see Barrett, a more recognizable Barrett, come with a few friends to watch his brother play ball.

Tyler shakes his helmeted head. His mother exhales a hostess's sigh, a dinner-party, the-soup-is-off sigh, which is audible even through the crowd noise. For Tyler, there is always this question: Why does she so baldly and winkingly impersonate somebody else? When will her deeper, subtler ambition be revealed?

Tyler says, "He never comes to the games."

"He never does, does he?"

"He's got other interests."

"He's a funny one, isn't he?" she answers.

It's difficult to imagine a less appropriate time for her to say something like that. Is she really announcing it to the parents of Harrisburg, to the cheerleaders and band members?

Tyler answers, "Yeah, kind of."

"Keep an eye on him, will you?"

"Uh, sure."

"I mean, I'd hate to see him get into trouble."

"What kind of trouble?"

She pauses, as if this particular question hasn't occurred to her until now.

"He shouldn't be some sort of oddity. He shouldn't be somebody who stays in his room all day, reading."

"He's okay," Tyler says. "I mean, he'll be okay."

"I hope you're right," she answers, and, with a regretful half-smile, settles back again into the chill October discomfort of her bleacher seat.

The pronouncement, it seems, has been made, and it apparently needs to have been made in an arena. Barrett is odd. Barrett is prone to defeat, and must be attended to.

Tyler trots back onto the field. He knows he has agreed to something. He can't quite figure out what. He suspects already, though, that he's offered more than he'll prove capable of delivering.

Now, more than twenty years later, this question: Has Tyler looked after Barrett too ardently? Has he disarmed Barrett by being the endlessly understanding big brother, the guy who never questions or criticizes?

Tyler pulls the tiny envelope out of his pocket.

Whoops, well, there's this secret too, isn't there?

It's for now, it's for this last song, and he can't really expect anyone, not *anyone*, to go along with it, not after he imploded (shoeless, muttering imprecations on Cornelia Street), not after the long and painfully serious talks with the hospital psychiatrist (who'd expected a woman with a bad dye job, and the hint of a limp?), not after rehab (at Barrett's and Liz's insistence), not now that his story has been so thoroughly reimagined.

And really, it's not a relapse. Not an actual relapse. He doesn't like this stuff, not all that much. He'd liked coke enormously, but coke was the wrong idea. With coke, he just kept trying to slap himself awake. Why didn't it occur to him that music comes from the land of nod? Music is the familiar strangeness of night visions—the half-feral boy cavorting on the path that winds through ancient trees, singing in what you understand to be a high and clear and not-quite-human voice, inaudible from the distance at which he performs his coltish, cloven-hoofed dance. The trick is to keep dreaming long enough to get within earshot.

Tyler has realized, he's come to understand, that he was mistaken about the writing of songs. It's one of those errors that lodges itself so deeply in your brain you can only think of how to get around it, without ever imagining that the idea itself might be wrong. Why didn't he figure this one out, years ago? You don't reach for music, you let music in. It's been a macho thing, all this time. He's been trying to wrestle the songs down, like some ridiculous, weaponless hunter who insists on catching birds in flight, with his bare hands, when what you do, lacking arrows, lacking a spear, is wait quietly, patiently, for the bird to alight.

Heroin is a better answer. Heroin lets more in. With heroin, Tyler can hear the sounds: Beth's last sick-animal moans; the low hum of his sorrows and self-recriminations; the even-lower hum of Earth itself, turning; the unshouted shout caught forever in Tyler's (in everybody's?) throat, that loud keening sound that has no actual meaning beyond the desire for more, the desire for less, the impossible foreignness of everything.

Never mind about the coming era. Get ready for it. Get ready for a heartless and shifty old president, for a vice president who thinks Africa is a country rather than a continent, who shoots wolves from helicopters.

With the heroin, Tyler can let that in. He can think about setting it to music.

The trick: to nip it at the lip of oblivion, without going over. To let the dark, gleaming entity into the room but keep it standing over there, on the other side, against the far wall; to insist that it wait, with all that sleep in its pockets, with those calm and compassionate eyes; to do just enough heroin to be able to see the figure, cloaked and kindly, but still hold it back, stave off the darkness it wants to bestow, so that the unwelcome sounds, the hospital moans, the distant shouts of brutal triumph, can still leak in and infect the air, without driving you insane. Without sending you barefoot onto Cornelia Street.

Tyler snorts two good ones (no needles, he's not a needles kind of guy), and seems, a moment later, to have stood up. It's funny. A little funny. He was lying on the sofa, and now he's standing up. He's standing in this empty room, where, it seems, he lives. There's music in his head, faint music, something of the bassoon about it; more throb than melody, but he could lay a melody on top of it; or no, not a melody (silly word) . . . a chant, Gregorian (kind of), he can hear that, too, a rumble of low voices, urgently contemplative, like rosary beads being read quickly but with infinite and practiced care; and then . . . something silvery, something soaring, a voice like a clarinet, singing in an unknown language; singing (it makes sense—somehow, it does) of hope and devastation, as if they were the same thing; as if, in the vocabulary of this language, there were only one word to convey the two conditions; as if hope implied destruction and destruction implied hope, so inevitably that they require only one name.

And then, it seems, he has opened one of the windows, and is sitting on the ledge.

Down there, between his dangling feet, is Avenue C, four stories below. There's a woman in a flowered dress, dragging an ancient schnauzer on a leash. There's another woman, in a purple dress (sisters?), rummaging through a garbage can. There's the sidewalk itself, the color of elephant hide, dotted with dark circles of long-discarded chewing gum. There's a hint of wind, bright wind, caressing the cuffs of his jeans.

He could slide off the sill. Couldn't he? It feels, at the moment, like he'd be slipping into a pool of water. There'd be that moment of impending relinquishment, threaded with hesitancy—will the water be cold? And then there'd be immersion.

He sits on the windowsill, looking down, with music playing in his head. He seems to be getting closer to the wild boy in the forest; close enough to be able to hear a hint of the boy's voice on the quickened air; close enough to begin to realize that it's not a boy after all, it's not exactly human, and there's something wrong with its face.

T he water in the harbor is going opaque with the nearly vanished sun, splashed here and there by the day's last orange-gold light, a light no longer brilliant; a light that feels old, as if it were beaming in from a past brighter than memory will allow it to have been but, nevertheless, dimmed slightly, inevitably, by the passing of decades. An enormous barge, the great brown-black floating platform of it (you could land a twin-engine plane on this one), has been turned copper by the last of the sun. The barge might be made of some semi-precious metal; a metal Barrett, standing at the stern of the ferry, can only think of as prosaically precious, sought after and coveted by industrialists, as opposed to kings.

Their mother was struck by lightning on a golf course. Why a comic tragedy? Barrett and Tyler have talked and talked about it. Why would a woman who'd been stern and intelligent; who'd been unpredictably generous or remote, depending on the hour (it's still hard to imagine anyone else as able to make so much sense to herself, and so little to others); who'd believed in good tailoring, worn coral lipstick, flirted imperiously with delivery boys, and been forthcoming (a little more so than Barrett might have liked) about her regrets (the house too far from town, the strand of inherited pearls stolen by a hotel maid—who else could it have been?), the decision to drop out of Bryn Mawr to marry their father (how could she have known, at the time, that New York would lead to Philadelphia, and Philadelphia to Harrisburg?); who'd been prone to get so absorbed in a book that she forgot to start dinner . . . Why that particular end, for her? Why an accident that could only be told as a sick joke? How is it possible that Betty Ferguson, her golf partner—Betty whom she had not particularly liked ("Betty is one of those women who believes her shoes and bag should match," "Betty is one of those women who looks more and more like a man as she ages")—was permitted to stand up at the memorial and announce that their mother had been three under par on that fateful day?

Barrett and Tyler aren't merely orphans, they're part of some horrible jest, have been since they were kids; they're the subjects of a god who seems to prefer jokes to the cleansing shock of wrath.

And here, now, spread before Barrett, is the rippling body of darkening water that so placidly received Beth's ashes.

There's an eye in the water. It's why Barrett keeps taking these ferry rides.

What's different about the eye in the water, what distinguishes it from that perceiving nocturnal roil of illumination, is the fact that Barrett has never seen it. He knows it's there, though. He knows that on these solitary rides, back and forth to Staten Island, he's being . . . apprehended. "Watched" isn't the right word. "Watched" implies a para-human intention Barrett does not feel from the restless and heavily trafficked harbor. But he felt it that first night, when Beth's ashes were consigned there. Beth joined the water, not in some fucked-up *her ghost is out there* way (screw that), but it seems that she, her mortal remains (which a vacuum cleaner could have sucked up in ten seconds), has joined an enormous cognizant unintelligence, and Barrett knows (is he going crazy, or is he going sane?), he knows it now and he knew it that night, that the world is inanimate but not unaware; that Beth is now part of something too majestic and vast to have thoughts or responses but is still, in its way, sentient.

It's delusional. It's probably delusional. But since Barrett helped to scatter Beth's ashes, he keeps returning to the harbor as if it were his true and heartless, inhuman parent, a parent that has no motives or ambitions on its children's behalf; that is neither proud nor disappointed. He can't shake the conviction that there's an eye in the water, never visible but always present, neither glad nor sorry to see him but alert somehow to the fact that he's come again.

Tyler found a mother for them, didn't he? This is a thought Barrett can contemplate only when he's riding the ferry. It might be true; it might not be. It has a ring of bullshit about it. But Beth was so different from Tyler's other girls. Tyler started up with her around the time Barrett's own life began to . . . *fall apart* is too melodramatic (Barrett, don't confuse yourself with a character in a B movie—or, for that matter, with someone out of Dostoyevsky) . . . to slide a little, to fail to coalesce, enough so that he had no choice but to move in with Tyler.

To move in with Tyler, and with Beth. Beth who was mild and kind, who was the same person every day. Beth who said, that night in the kitchen on New Year's Eve, that Barrett and Tyler should know about the dimming of the house lights, they should know that there comes a time when the question of good versus bad ceases to matter.

Is it possible, even remotely so, that Barrett's true ambition in life turns out to have been insisting on himself as Tyler's little brother?

Boats against the current, borne back ceaselessly into the past. Fuck you, F. Scott Fitzgerald.

Say it, then. Say it to yourself. When Beth recovered, you believed you knew—you suspected you knew—what the light had meant to tell you: that you've reproduced your childhood with Tyler, and that this woman, this time, will not attract the attention of the jokester god.

Which would imply that the light had lied. And that the water is telling the truth.

·

An hour later, after Barrett has made the round-trip to Staten Island, Sam is waiting for him, just as he said he would, uptown, in the park, at Bethesda Fountain. Barrett sees him from the balustrade that hovers thirty feet or so above the fountain's plaza. Sam sits on the fountain's lip, under the angel—the peasant-girl angel, sturdy and strapping, looking not ecstatically skyward but gravely down, earth-entranced, from her platter of bronze, skeins of water spilling out around her as she extends one arm and holds, with the other, her spear of lilies.

Barrett stands for a while on the balustrade above the fountain. He can see Sam, but Sam can't see him. He can observe an interlude of private Sam-ness, the Sam who doesn't know Barrett is there; the Sam who exists privately, who doesn't alter his demeanor (if he does so at all) for Barrett's sake.

Sam sits solidly, feet planted on the bricks, hands on knee-caps, as if he were resting briefly from some strenuous labor that will continue after this short, union-mandated rest period. He's like a guy taking a break. He's wearing the carpenter's jeans to which he's so devoted, and the gray corduroy Carhartt jacket Barrett gave him for his birthday last week, a jacket Sam likes better than Barrett does (it's a love sign, isn't it, the ability to give a gift the receiver wants more than you do?); Sam harboring, as he does, this particular devotion to workingman's modesty, this obscure desire to be mistakable for a construction worker, when in fact he teaches nineteenth-century English and American literature at Princeton.

Sam comports himself as if he's visiting from another planet, where the standards are different, and where he's considered a prize. On Sam's planet, the coveted features include an overly large head, with gray eyes set disconcertingly far apart; a mere parenthesis of a nose (which enhances the enormous-head effect); and a wide, equine mouth above a chin so broad and horsey that it's possible to imagine holding a lump of sugar out in your hand for him to nuzzle curiously and then, with a gentle scrape of whiskers against your palm, accept.

Sam walks through the world with such unapologetic

certainty that, although no one has ever called him hand-some, almost everyone who knows him has called him, in one way or another, surprisingly sexy.

He and Barrett met, just five months ago, in a Korean deli on lower Broadway. They were browsing the cooler, which was curtained, in that slightly upsetting way, by those verti-cal bands of clear plastic that imply some remote and impov-erished clinic, short on medicine, able to keep flies away from the mortally ill, but not much beyond that.

Barrett and Sam started talking about the merits of Coke versus Pepsi.

One Tuesday you're headed home, and you think, I'm going to stop in this deli to which I've never gone before, and get a Coke. One Tuesday, at six thirty-two. There's this big guy standing at the cooler, you don't think much of him one way or another, so it's natural, it requires no courage or effort, to ask, "Are you Coke, or Pepsi?" It is not surprising that the guy turns to look at you, that he offers a contempla-tive little smile, as if it had been an actual, serious question, and says, "Pepsi. No question. Coke is the Beatles, Pepsi is the Rolling Stones."

And then it's only semi-surprising that you see kindly gray depths in his eyes, that you see a resigned weariness in them, that you imagine—thinking nothing will come of it—that you imagine for some reason how you might sit with his head in your lap, stroking his gunmetal hair (defiantly unwashed) and telling him, Rest, just rest for a minute.

Sam is not Barrett's type (although Barrett would, until they met, have insisted that he had no "type" at all). Sam is neither young nor briskly, foolishly optimistic; he is not a broad-shouldered pugilist; he is not anyone Eakins would have wanted to paint.

Love, it seems, arrives not only unannounced, but so accidentally, so randomly, as to make you wonder why you, why anyone, believes even fleetingly in laws of cause and effect.

Barrett remains a little longer at the balustrade, watching Sam. When will this one, Barrett wonders, send him off with an e-mail or a text? Or will this one simply stop returning calls entirely? It is, after all, a tradition, for Barrett. It keeps refusing not to happen.

Barrett thinks—he thinks, briefly—of turning around and leaving the park; of being, this time, the vanisher, the man who leaves you wondering, who offers no explanation, not even the sour satisfaction of a real fight; who simply drifts away, because (it seems) there's affection and there's sex but there's no urgency, no little hooks clasping little eyes; no bindings, no dogged devotions, no prayers for mercy, not when mercy can be so easily self-administered. What would it be like, Barrett wonders, to be the other, the man who's had the modest portion he thinks of as enough, who slips away before the mess sets in, before he's available to accusation and recrimination, before the authorities start demanding of him When, and Why, and With Whom?

Beth had just over five months. Out of nowhere. She was granted three months and four days until it came raging back, and among Barrett's regrets (he cultivates what he likes to consider an appropriate number of them) is the fact that she got so sick again, so quickly, there was never a moment, never a proper moment, in which to ask her whether she'd been grateful for the reprieve.

She must have been grateful. Barrett insists that she was. Didn't she say so, more or less, on New Year's Eve? If not in actual words, didn't she let him, him and Tyler, know that she was glad to be held between them at a party but that she knew (it does seem, in retrospect, that she knew) she was a species of ghost, permitted by some fluke in the system to haunt in corporeal form, which must—mustn't it?—have been a pleasure for her. Unless it wasn't; unless, when the cancer came back, she felt doubly betrayed, mistreated, fucked with.

Sam will, in all likelihood, leave, either sooner or later. No one yet has failed to. But there is, in fact, so little time. Barrett straightens up, starts toward the stairs that lead down to the little plaza in which the angel stands with her endless bronze patience, where Sam is waiting.

After she's closed the shop, Liz can't seem to go home. It's too corny, it's too old-ladyish, to think of herself as dreading her empty apartment—who'd want to entertain that visitation of pathos?—but still, after she's closed up, she wanders through Williamsburg on one of the last warm evenings in November. The bars and restaurants on Driggs put out their golden glows (these places all know about lighting), packed with celebrants, their entrances crowded with loiterers whose names are on the list, who wait, laughing and smoking, on the sidewalk. Everyone is twenty-four years old.

It's a land of the young, which could of course be depressing to Liz, though as she walks unnoticed along Driggs, she's aware—tonight, more than ever—of how temporarily young these denizens are; how ephemeral is this night of theirs; how soon they'll be reminiscing, as toddlers tumble around their living room floors, about *those nights in Williamsburg*. Maybe it's their youthful promise and prosperity, the clear abundance of their gifts that will . . . not undo them, not that exactly, but tame them, urge them homeward, bring them to their senses. They are not (not, at least, most of them, as far as Liz can tell) prone to the extraordinary—they have moved so eagerly to Williamsburg, so willingly worn its clothes. It would be silly, it would be churlish, for Liz to disparage as she walks invisibly among them; it would be mean-spirited not to convey to them, telepathically, her hope that they survive as gracefully as possible the day the cord starts tightening (we need a bigger place, now that the baby is almost two), the year they understand that they're charming eccentrics now, still working in computer graphics or as sound technicians, not by any means unrecognizable to themselves but members (surprise) of the rest of the aging population, the latest version (hipster version) of the forty-year-olds who still sport a few vestiges of punk, the fifty-year-olds (that's you, Liz) who still work, in a modified way, that thrift-store cowgirl-hooker thing.

She can't go home, not yet. But she can't wander through Williamsburg either, not much longer.

She turns down Fifth Street, and walks toward the Williamsburg Bridge.

She knows, of course she knows, where she's going. What's strange is she hasn't decided on it. She's simply going, as if it were inevitable, as if there were nowhere else.

·

Avenue C, in the early evening, is the slightly more foolish cousin of Driggs. Here, too, are crowded, prospering bars and cafés, though fewer of them—Liz walks an entire block and passes only a fluorescent deli, a Chinese take-out joint, a Laundromat (LAST WASH 9 P.M.), a tattoo parlor (no customers, at the moment), a bicycle repair place already shuttered for the night, and the vacant remains of what had been a pet shop (its window still bearing, in silver letters, the words CANARIES AND OTHER SONGBIRDS), but the young people in these bars and cafés (most of them undergraduates, out for the evening in what they consider an edgy neighborhood) are more like the daughters and sons of minor aristocrats— charming, lazy, well-fed children who dress stylishly but are not in costume; who neither expect nor court surprise. A boy in a faux-ratty blazer (Ralph Lauren, Liz can always spot it) leans out of a tavern doorway and shouts, to his cigarette-smoking friends, "They just scored another one."

Liz reaches the building, its blank, cordovan-colored brick facade, and rings 4B. No answer. She rings one more time.

It's just as well. She's been spared the indignity. It's time for her to hail a cab and go home.

As she's turning to leave, though—Tyler's voice, from above.

"Hey."

Liz passes through a moment of impossibility. Tyler is speaking to her from the sky; Tyler has died, he's hovering above the earthly plane . . .

She looks up. Tyler is standing on the fourth-floor windowsill, semi-visible above the light-layer put out by the streetlamps, like a carving in a niche on the high wall of a church.

Liz shouts, "What in the fuck are you doing?"

Tyler doesn't answer. He looks down with benign patience at her, looks past her at the sparse traffic on Avenue C.

"Get down from there," Liz shouts.

After a moment's hesitation—a barely agitated pause, as if he were reluctant to reveal a confidence—Tyler says, "I'm not going to jump."

"You'd fucking better not. Get down from there and buzz me in."

Tyler looks at her again, with an expression of regretful compassion Liz remembers from a particular angel—it must have been a sculpture from the church of her childhood.

"Do it now," Liz says.

Slowly, with lazy resignation, Tyler withdraws from the window. Soon after, the buzzer sounds, and Liz hurries inside.

The door to the apartment is unlocked. The apartment is dark. Liz finds Tyler returned to where she left him, hours and hours ago. He's lying on the sofa in an attitude of ordinary recumbency. Liz suppresses an urge to stride over and slap him, as hard as she's able to, across the face.

"What was *that* about?" she asks.

"I'm sorry if I scared you," he answers.

"What were you *doing*?"

"I'm not really sure. I wanted to get out of the apartment but not go down to the street."

"You really weren't going to jump?"

"No. I mean, I thought about it. I was *thinking* about jumping, I wasn't *going* to. There's a difference, right?"

"I suppose there is."

How is it possible that this makes sense to her?

He says, "We've been having sex for years."

"I know."

"And we've never said anything about it. Not anything at all."

"I know that, too."

"Does that seem odd to you?"

"I don't know," she says. "Yeah, I guess."

"We were sneaking around on Beth. And Andrew."

"Did it really feel like sneaking around, to you?"

"I don't know," he says. "Would Andrew have minded?"

"No. Well. If he'd minded, he couldn't have let himself. Minding would have been too . . . Not who Andrew wanted to be."

"Do you miss him?" Tyler asks.

"No."

"Does *that* seem odd, to you?"

"Oh, well, sure, there are things. There are things I miss. Mostly the nasty stuff, to be perfectly frank. A twenty-eight-year-old, in bed . . . Oh, never mind. But really, the drug business got to be a little much."

"He did like his drugs, didn't he? But you did, too."

"Oh, I liked a coked-out night every now and then. Andrew was a lot more . . . urgent about it."

"As people sometimes are."

"And who," she says, "those last months, do you think was *paying* for them?"

"I guess I must have assumed."

"It wasn't the money, really. It just started to make me feel. Well . . . Peeling off twenties for your much-younger lover's dealer. That's an experience you can skip. Trust me."

"I do," he says. "Trust you."

"Beth wouldn't have minded, either. If I'd thought she would, I'd never have gone near you."

"But still. You never told her."

"It wasn't because of you," she says.

"And so, it was because . . ."

"It was because I didn't think she needed another reminder that she was dying, and somebody had to take over for her. In certain ways."

Tyler changes, though he doesn't move.

"Is that what you were doing?" he asks. "Taking over one of Beth's duties for her?"

"Honestly? Yes. At first."

"You were pinch-hitting for a girlfriend."

"That was at first. It got different, after a while."

"I'm forty-seven. I look it."

Liz says, "I'm fifty-six. You're actually a little young for me."

"I was kind of a pretty kid. That's how I came into the world. It's a little off-putting, actually. I mean, being this guy people don't really look at anymore."

"I look at you."

"I don't mean you. I mean strangers. People for whom looking at you is optional."

"It matters to me," she says, "that you took such good care of Beth."

"I only did what anyone would."

"You haven't been around much, have you?"

"I feel like I've been around."

"You didn't recoil from her. I saw it. You watched death eat her up, not just once but twice, and you didn't lose your hold on her. You didn't stop recognizing her."

"It was just . . . I mean, who wouldn't have?"

"A lot of people. I walked here, by the way."

"From Williamsburg?"

"Yep. I walked across the bridge."

"Why?"

"Why were you standing on the window ledge?"

"Answer the question, please."

"I am," she says. "I had this urge to walk all the way to your place. You had an urge to be outside, but not on the street. Both of us, at the same time. Do you see the connection?"

"Sort of. Actually, no. Not really."

"Should I go?"

"No," he says. "Would you come and lie here with me for a while? I'm not putting a move on."

"It would be okay if you were."

"It's just so dark in here."

"You don't have any *lights*. Did you and Barrett really get rid of *everything*?"

"Not the sofa. Not the TV."

"The only two objects in the world that mean anything to you."

"It'd just be nice to lie here for a while, could we do that?"

"Yes," she says. "We could."

T he streetlamps in the park emit wan circles, skirts of light, with a thin, agitated darkness between them. Sam says to Barrett, "It's not for the whole evening, right?"

Barrett has been checking the sky as they walk. He can't seem to help it; not when he's in Central Park. It is, as usual, the usual sky.

"No," he says. "I wouldn't inflict an entire evening of Andrew and Stella on you. It's just that, you know. He called."

Sam says, "Central Park was always meant for the rich. Did you know that?"

"I think I've heard it, somewhere."

"In the mid–eighteen hundreds, they laid out the future

New York. This was all just woods and farms then, up here."

"I know. I do know that."

"There were those who favored the London model. Lots of little parks, everywhere. They lost. The guys who won pushed through this gigantic park that was miles away from where poor people lived. And they told Frederick Law Olmsted, nothing that poor people like. No parade grounds, no ball fields."

"Really?" Barrett says.

"As you can imagine, real estate values soared. The poor were downtown, the rich were uptown. And here we are."

"Here we are."

"I'm being pedantic, aren't I?" Sam says. "Am I boring you?"

"No," Barrett answers. "I'm kind of pedantic, too."

Barrett permits himself a good, long look at Sam, as they walk. Sam's face, in profile, is more stern and conventionally handsome than is his face seen frontally. Viewed from the side, his nose has more consequence; the dome of his forehead meets, with a more powerful, architectural curve, the wild rags of his hair. In profile he looks, ever so slightly, like Beethoven.

Don't the Japanese have a word for this? Is it *ma*? It means (does it actually exist in Japanese, or is it merely something Barrett has invented, and tried to dignify by way of an Asian aesthetic?) that which can't be seen in any fixed or singular way; that which changes as you move through it. Buildings have *ma*. Gardens have it. Sam has it.

Sam says, "What is it?"

"Nothing."

Sam laughs. He comes equipped with a deep, musical laugh—the woodwind section, tuning up before the concert begins.

·

Andrew and Stella are waiting for them in Strawberry Fields. They sit together, huddled close, on a bench near the lip of the Imagine disk. They are like penniless young travelers, neither desperate nor defeated (not yet), but growing tired, by now, of their wanderings; passing through that youthful moment in which fecklessness starts, ever so slightly, to curdle; not yet possessed of a destination but beginning to want one, which is surprising to them—they'd believed they were the ones who'd slip through, who'd be vagabonds forever, who'd be happy with panhandled change, Dumpster diving, the occasional night spent sleeping, as best they could, in the waiting room of a bus depot somewhere. Andrew and Stella are like young lovers who are just now realizing—to their sad astonishment—that their mothers' calls (*Baby, it's late, it's time to come home now*) are no longer the vexations they'd always been; that those imprecations are turning— the last thing either of them wants—into kindness; that their mothers' voices and their mothers' concern for safety and comfort are taking on a gravitational pull.

Andrew and Stella have been talking to each other with sufficient, soft-voiced intensity that they seem to be surprised when Barrett and Sam stride up.

"Hey," Barrett calls.

Andrew turns, grins mightily at Barrett. "Hey, man," he says.

Is it possible that Andrew has aged? It's not possible.

Barrett saw him mere months ago. His face is still that of a marble in a museum. But something is changing. Is it? Is some ravishment starting to fester under his skin, not yet visible on the surface, but about to be? Is some aspect of early, gaunt ruin preparing to arrive? Or is it just the dimness of the light?

Stella smiles knowingly at Barrett, as if she's just barely suppressing laughter. Stella could be the daughter of a dreamy young goddess who managed, somehow, to mate with a falcon. She's birdlike, but sharply and fiercely so. Her tiny frame—her milkily skinny arms, the long white stem of her neck—conveys a raptor's deft acuity. She is small but not, in any way, fragile.

Andrew leaps up from the bench, offers Barrett his customary victor's handshake, the shoulder-height presentation of open palm, which Barrett returns. Andrew administers the same shake to Sam, whom he has met once, briefly, accidentally, on Orchard Street.

Sam says, "Hey there, Andrew."

Stella does not rise from the bench. Barrett goes to her, as he is clearly expected to.

"Hello, Stella," he says.

She trains her falcon eyes on him. Her eyes aren't menacing, not exactly menacing—Barrett is not her prey. She does, however, make it clear that she sees him, sees everything, from a considerable height, that she can spot a rabbit's shadow as clearly as most people see the lights of an approaching train.

"Hi, Barrett," she says. Her voice, high-pitched, girlishly offhand, does not match the rest of her. A softer, simpler girl speaks from the raptor's face and body. Who knows which is the truer?

Andrew, the host of this small, mysterious party, says, "Thanks for coming, you guys."

"Hey, it's a nice night," Barrett says. "It's one of the last ones. I mean, that low rumble you hear? It's winter. It's only about a mile away."

"Yeah, totally," Andrew says.

Barrett is aware of Sam, standing quietly, wondering, in all likelihood, what exactly he's doing here; how this has happened to him.

"So," Barrett says. "Should we go somewhere for a drink, maybe?"

"We don't really go to bars," Stella says.

"Well, then," Barrett says. "What if Sam and I go get us a bottle of wine or something, and bring it back?"

"We don't drink," Stella says.

Barrett says, "Oh, well, that's good. Drink is bad for you. I myself drink, I admit it, and just look at my life."

Stella stares with predator's attention at him, as if he has made a literal statement. It would seem that she, like Andrew, does not speak irony or wit—it's a dialect unknown in their region.

Barrett glances over at Sam, promises him, with his eyes, that he'll get them out of here as soon as it's humanly possible.

Stella says softly, more in Barrett's direction than to Barrett himself, "You're going to see something miraculous."

Barrett turns back to her. He's aware of her physical insubstantiality, a quality that's not delicate or frail but ever so slightly translucent, as if her flesh itself were made of a substance more pliable, more prone to bruises and scars, than that of most people. It's as if she has not quite thoroughly, physically imagined herself.

Barrett asks, "What do you mean?"

Stella's expression of vague semi-attention does not change, nor does the low, incantatory aspect of her voice.

She says, "You're going to see something miraculous. Soon."

"What do you think it is?" Barrett asks.

She shakes her head. "I have no idea," she says. "I'm just a little bit psychic."

With that, she returns from what had been . . . not a trance, nothing nearly that dramatic; she returns from her stoner's aspect of fixation on the empty air that hovers before her eyes.

They're high, aren't they, she and Andrew. How could Barrett have failed to notice it? He's had, God knows, enough practice with Tyler.

"That'll be nice," he says. "I look forward to that."

Andrew breaks in. He might be a bored husband at a dinner party, some guy who's finally had his fill of girlish banter and decides, with a certain glad-handing force, to bring up the question of asphalt versus wood shingles, or the superior virtues of his sound system.

He says to Barrett, "Man, okay. There's something I want to tell you. And, you know, I didn't want to say it over the phone."

"What is it?" Barrett asks.

"And I thought, hey, what better place to tell you than Central Park."

"Great. Let's hear it."

Andrew glances at Stella and Sam, tentatively but conspiratorially—*Don't worry, these people are okay, these people can be trusted.*

He says to Barrett, "I saw the light. I mean, the one you told me about."

Barrett has nothing to offer by way of an answer. He looks again in Sam's direction. Sam has no idea about the light. Sam seems to find himself among foreigners, who speak a language he doesn't understand, and so his only option is to stand, cordially half-smiling, wearing an expression of benign semi-comprehension.

"Last night," Andrew says. "I was coming home. I was just, you know, walking along Utica. We live in Crown Heights now."

Stella says, with proud defiance, "We live in this humongous apartment. With a whole bunch of people. Nice people." She might be defending the virtues—the simple customs, the deeper humanity—of a small, internationally negligible, country.

"Right."

"I looked up," Andrew says. "It was like, something told me to look up. And there it was."

"The light," Barrett says.

"It was kind of . . . twinkly," Andrew says. "It was right there. Like this little handful of stars. But lower than stars. Green. Closer to, you know, the earth. Than stars are."

"You really saw it," Barrett says.

"He did," Stella says. *Do not doubt the word of my mate.*

"I wanted to tell you that," Andrew says to Barrett. "I saw it too, man. And hey, what better place to tell you than here in the park?"

"That's . . . amazing."

"It was totally beautiful."

"Yeah."

Barrett is surprised to realize that he's trembling. Is it possible? Yes, it is. It might be possible. Wasn't Andrew the first person he told? Didn't some instinct compel him? He'd thought it was lust, and cocaine. But maybe, maybe, he knew, he somehow knew, that Andrew, simple beautiful Andrew, was the only person of his acquaintance who might be . . . innocent enough to believe him. Who might, as it now seems, be innocent enough to see the light, himself.

There was Liz, too, of course, but Liz insisted then, and insists today, that it was imaginary.

A new, improved reality begins, tentatively, to assert itself. There exists, on earth, a small cohort of ordinary citizens (hasn't God always favored the ordinary citizens?) who are prone to visions.

What if Barrett (and Andrew, and maybe even cynical Liz) are on the brink of revelation; what if they're among the first to know that their maker is coming back for them?

It's possible. It does not, at the moment, seem impossible.

Barrett manages to keep his voice steady. He says to Andrew, "So. A little handful of stars."

"Yeah. Kind of turquoise."

"And did you . . . *feel* something?"

"I felt the eye of God, man. Just kind of checking me out."

Yes. Wow. These straggly pilgrims, receivers of a celestial wink . . .

Barrett says, haltingly, "I know. I mean, I felt it, too. This . . . watchfulness. Aimed at you."

"Totally."

"This is . . . This is amazing."

"It's totally amazing."

A silence passes. Barrett does his best to remember Sam,

poor Sam, standing aside, wondering *what the hell*, but Sam will understand, he'll have to, Barrett will explain it all to him. Barrett isn't crazy, he's not deluded. Some gigantic, hitherto unknown parent has decided it's time to let the children know that they're seen, they're accounted for; they haven't, after all, been lost in the forest all this time . . .

"So, listen," Andrew says. "I've got a little favor to ask."

"Okay. Sure. Anything."

Andrew pauses, produces the grin again, that immaculate smile, devoid of artifice or intention; just pure boy-delight.

He says, "I've got a little problem going on. A little bit of a problem."

"What is it?"

"It's kind of about money."

"Oh." Barrett can't seem to register anything but "oh," and can't seem to inflect that monosyllable with anything better than puzzled disappointment.

Andrew withdraws the grin. There's something unsettling about it, the swiftness with which he's able to make it disappear. His face darkens. Here, again, is that aspect of nascent ravishment, of a condition about to exhibit its first, subtle symptoms—the rash on the verge of surfacing, the cough deeper and damper than an ordinary cough.

Andrew says. "I owe a guy some money."

"I see."

Barrett waits, he can only wait. Something terrible is coming, he can feel it, a tidal surge; a strange, opaque greening of the water on what's been, until this moment, a summer day at the beach.

"I got a little carried away," Andrew says. "You know how you can get carried away, right?"

"I do."

"And this guy. He kind of wants some money from me. That I owe him."

There's a guy to whom Andrew owes money. The guy probably wants it sooner, as opposed to later.

"I see," Barrett says.

"So I was wondering. Do you think you could loan me a few bucks?"

"Loan you a few bucks."

"I mean, we've both seen the light."

Barrett can't seem to answer. He's not ready, not quite, to enter this new revelation—this un-revelation. It's a scam. Andrew hasn't seen anything in the sky. Andrew is merely hustling. He's chosen Barrett as his mark because Barrett is prone to delusion, Barrett is a zealot of sorts, Andrew has always been exquisitely aware of his effect on Barrett (why would anyone imagine that beautiful children live unaware of it?), Barrett will contribute to the Guys Who've Seen a Light Foundation.

Stella has been put up to it. Stella has been instructed: toss him a psychic "prediction," so you can claim surprise when you learn that you had the phenomenon right but the time wrong.

"You're my friend, right?" Andrew says. "I'm in a little bit of a fix, right now, I mean I need a friend."

Barrett hears himself say, "I don't really have any money. I don't exactly *make* any money. I work in Liz's shop."

And then, on Andrew's face—a look of haggard desperation. A version of his face Barrett has never seen before. Andrew is, suddenly, the haunted one, yearning from a front porch on a hot August day, watching the world stroll by, astonished by its apparent ability to do so well without him.

"Man," he says, "I'm not talking about a lot of money. I'm in trouble, here. Do you get that?"

"I do," Barrett answers. "I get it. I don't think I can help you, though."

"I saw a *light*. I got the wink of holiness. That matters, between us, it's got to matter, right?"

"You didn't really see anything, did you?"

"Man, I just told you . . ."

Sam says, "How much do you need?"

The coffee shop is a box of strident light. Tyler holds his coffee mug in both hands, enfolds it. Liz ignores entirely her little pot of tea.

"Can you believe I've never been to California?" Tyler says.

"All kinds of people have never been to California."

This particular coffee shop, on one of the darker blocks of Avenue C, is patronized by people for whom it seems things aren't quite working out. A woman with blindingly orange hair asks more loudly than necessary what the soup of the day is. Two men, both wearing sunglasses, argue about whether there's a difference between cement and concrete.

"There's a town called Castroville," Tyler says to Liz. "It's the artichoke capital of the world."

"That's the main attraction, for you?"

"No. It just seems so . . . California."

"I suppose it does."

"Every year they have an artichoke festival. There's a parade. There's a queen. They dress her up in a gown made of artichoke leaves. And guess who was once the artichoke queen? Marilyn Monroe."

"Where do you *get* things like this?"

"I'm a news junkie."

"This was on the *news*?"

"We'd be in California for the election," he says.

"We would."

"Maybe it'd work out so we'd be at the artichoke festival, we'd be watching a girl parading down some little street in a gown made of artichoke leaves when we find out it's McCain and Palin."

"That would be a big coincidence, don't you think?"

"Sure. I just feel like, I don't know, there'd be some sort of fucked-up comfort if it were possible to find out that the country was finally, really and truly going to destroy itself while we were watching a pretty girl in a dress made of artichoke leaves, waving at a crowd."

"You're obsessed."

"Uh, excuse me? 'Obsessed' is for minor passions. Obsessed is people with seventeen cats. Obsessed is people who own every video game ever produced, since Pong. I'm interested in the fate of the world. Does that strike you as eccentric?"

She says, "If you were coming to California with me, I'd need you to stop doing drugs."

"I'm not doing drugs."

All she has to do is level her eyes at him.

"You think you know everything, don't you?" he says.

"No. I just always assume the worst, and sometimes it looks as if I know everything."

From three booths away, one of the men in sunglasses says, "Cement has a higher sand content. That's why all those buildings in backward countries collapse. They use cement."

Tyler gazes into the black circle of his coffee. He says, "I'm done with drugs. Really and truly."

"You're lying."

"I'm not."

"Well, then. That's good."

She knows, of course she knows, that he's lying.

"When I *was* doing drugs," Tyler says, "it was to get to the music. I couldn't seem to do it with my naked unaltered brain."

"Do you have any idea what an *addict* statement that is?" Liz asks.

"Right. I know. It's so much better, all clean and sober-like."

"That's the general idea. Among the population at large."

Tyler says, "The thing is. When you're doing drugs. There's this feeling that you're trying to find a way to get to the place where the music is."

One of the sunglasses-wearing men, the other one, says, "You're crazy. It's just two words for the same thing."

"I understand that," Liz says. "I used to do drugs to feel connected to Andrew. By way of example."

"Uh, right. Me trying to write a decent song is like you trying to get through an evening with a boy who'd need a minute to tell his right hand from his left."

"Okay. Bad example. I'm just trying to tell you something about how, if you were doing drugs again, I'd understand. I'd still want you to stop. But I'd understand."

Tyler nods, as if agreeing to an old truism he secretly knows to be false.

This would be the moment to tell Liz the truth.

The moment passes.

"I'm done, though," Tyler says. "I'm all done. It's rough. I mean, I'm alone with the music now."

She says, "What if that mattered less?"

"Come again?"

"What if your whole life wasn't about writing songs?"

"I don't like the sound of that, frankly."

"I don't mean give it up. I mean, what if you were a man who's living a life, and writing songs is part of it?"

He says, "Step away, devil."

She laughs. She knows enough to laugh.

The orange-haired woman announces to the waitress that she'll try the cabbage soup, but warns her of the very real possibility that she'll feel compelled to send it back.

Liz says, "You thought you could write music that would save Beth's life. Don't you think so?"

"That would be delusions of grandeur."

"Or it would be some kind of frankly very touching idea you've got that you can do more than human beings can actually do."

The first of the sunglasses men says, "Why would there be two different words for the same thing? That doesn't make sense."

Tyler says, "There's this thing I've been thinking, lately."

"Mmm-hmm."

"It's not even a real *thought*, exactly. I mean, I haven't

phrased it, not even to myself. It's like the still-forming molecule of a thought."

"Too new to talk about?"

"I'm going to take a shot at it."

"By all means."

"I've been wondering," he says, "if trying to write songs matters more to me than the songs themselves."

"I get that."

"Do you?"

"Yes. I think I do."

"It's like, what I really love is the anticipation. I love the idea of the song. Then, when it's finished . . ."

"Even your YouTube hit?"

"Even that. It feels sort of . . . disembodied. Like an artifact from some lost civilization nobody misses all that much."

"It is, in fact, a good song," she says. "Just FYI."

The orange-haired woman says, to no one in particular, that cabbage sometimes gives her gas.

"That doesn't seem to matter, exactly," Tyler says. "I still have to finish the album. One more song to go."

"Maybe you won't finish the album."

"I have a contract."

"Who gives a shit about a contract?"

He nods. Who does, in fact, give a shit about a contract?

She says, "There are redwood forests in California."

"So I've heard."

"There are waves crashing up against cliffs, with eagles circling in the sky."

"I've seen pictures."

"But that doesn't mean we couldn't go to Castroville,

too," she says. "If you really want to see a girl in a dress made of artichoke leaves."

"I can't go," Tyler says. "Not now. I've got to finish the album."

He places his hand, palm down, on the tabletop. Liz looks, scrutinizingly, at his hand.

"That's what you should do, then," she says. "You could meet me in California later. If you want to."

"And we could go to Castroville. For the artichoke festival."

"We could. I mean, we'd have to find out when it is. That would matter."

"Very Google-able," he answers.

"I'll be in California," she says. "I'll let you know where to find me."

"That's good. That's good to know."

After a moment, she puts her own hand on top of his, as the waitress arrives to ask, with an ancient and grudging cordiality, if they're finished, or if they'd care for refills.

As they make their way across the Great Lawn, Barrett asks Sam, "Why would you give money to Andrew?"

"It sounds like he needs it," Sam says. "And I've got money. A little, not a lot. But I've got enough to keep some foolish boy from getting whacked by a drug dealer."

"Do you really think somebody would *whack* Andrew?"

"I have no idea. That's not what matters, is it?"

"What is it that matters?"

"Someone needs a little money. You seem to have a little money. And so, maybe you could help."

"Even if it's just a scam?" Barrett asks.

"I think pretty much everybody who says he needs

money really and truly needs money. Maybe not for the reasons he's telling you. But still."

"That's sort of Christian."

"It's just human. Not that Christians aren't welcome to it. But it's not as if they own it."

"They own a lot," Barrett says.

"The real estate holdings alone are mind-boggling. Argh, I'm being pedantic again."

"And as we know, I like pedantic. I know pedantic. I *live* pedantic."

Impulsively, childishly, Barrett pinches the sleeve of Sam's jacket between his fingers. Locating himself, as a child might.

Is it possible that Sam is possessed of simple kindness and generosity—that those qualities are real, and enduring? Is it possible that that might matter, that it might sustain, that it might be a rope you could hold on to, going hand over hand, toward a destination still too distant to be visible?

They traverse the Great Lawn. Ahead of them looms the vast limestone bulk of the Metropolitan Museum, its stern, familiar brightness. Barrett thinks, as he always does when he approaches the museum, of what lies within: a more-than-adequate sampling of every instance in which human beings were inspired to do more than human beings can technically do, whether it's the summoning of life from the stubborn inanimacy of paint and canvas, or the hammering of gold into reliquary saints with ecstatic and tortured faces the size of dimes.

Up ahead is the place where Barrett saw the light. Barrett and Sam may be about to walk more or less exactly across the spot on which Barrett stood when the light manifested itself.

Maybe Liz is correct. Maybe the light was merely a hallucination, created from some confluence of constellation and airplane, invented by Barrett on a night when he so urgently needed to feel more accompanied in the world.

Or maybe the light was actually looking at the museum, acknowledging its slumbering, nocturnal wonders, and Barrett assumed the light to be regarding *him*, the way one returns enthusiastically the smile and wave of a stranger who is in fact smiling and waving at someone standing behind you.

Or maybe the light was just another of God's jokes. Maybe Barrett should consider refusing to fall for this one.

Sam says, "Do you want to tell me what all that was about a light?"

"It's a whole strange story," Barrett tells him.

"I like strange stories."

"You do, right?" he asks. "You do like strange stories."

"I can't really think of a story that'd be too strange."

"That's good," Barrett says.

This surprise: Barrett is, for the first time in memory, not the one who hopes, perhaps a bit too eagerly, to charm; who searches his mind for interesting stories (and then worries that the stories are too self-consciously "interesting"); who attempts, by various means, to explain his own life to another, while plucking a bouquet of roses from his sleeve. He is not only the one yearning to be kissed; he also inspires that yearning in another.

Coke or Pepsi? The most banal of all possible mock-questions, asked of a stranger who did not seem, at the time, to matter much at all. Who could have imagined an answer this long, this complicated?

Barrett waits a moment before he speaks. Sam glances

over at him as they walk. Sam's eyes are benign, intelligent, and, at the moment, more than a little impassive. Sam has, after all, been told he's about to hear a strange story, and despite his assurances that he likes his stories strange (what else, exactly, was he going to say?), he must be feeling wary. Who knows what strange stories he's been told by other men? Who can tell how fearful he is? How lurid is his own history of dismissals and vanishings; of stories that turn out to be just slightly too strange to bear?

Barrett fixes his own eyes on Sam's. A living silence passes between them; a brief interlude of quiet during which the very molecules of the air feel as if they're more agitated than usual, more alive with some sort of invisible spark, some barely audible buzz. Barrett walks alongside Sam. Barrett feels charged, as if his ON switch is on; as if he emanates heat and a cloudy but palpable, slightly feverish light.

Stella's phrase returns to him. *You're going to see something miraculous.* Is it possible, could it be, that she actually is a little bit psychic; that she's not a crook; that she sensed something actual; that she was referring to the future and not the past; that Barrett is in fact about to see something miraculous, though there's no way to determine its nature?

He gathers himself, re-collects himself, gets himself ready to give it, once again. The whole thing: the hopes designed to be trampled; the image of a new life that's probably not much more than clownish optimism. He devotes his whole attention to the still largely unknown man who walks beside him, waiting. Barrett swears he sees, on Sam's face, an expression of quizzical, nervously anticipated recognition; a premonition on Sam's part that nothing about Barrett could be too much, or too little. Barrett does not look up at the sky.

It's just Tyler now, on the sofa in the otherwise-empty apartment (discounting the blind gleam of the TV screen) (in mere days, that glossy, glassy rectangle—let's not kid ourselves—will show Sarah Palin, grinning in triumph, confetti caught in her hair). But here, for now, there's the blank silence of the television; the velvet loveliness of the dark and the quiet (discounting the cars rumbling by outside, and the woman shouting—to whom?—"You never ever ever ever ever . . .").

The world is ending. McCain and Palin will see to that. Tyler feels (he admits it) a minor, queasy satisfaction, in the pit of his stomach: he has, at least, been right, all along.

Even the coming collapse, however, feels remote, at present. Tyler has put himself back into floatation mode, thanks to his sidekick, the friend in the strangely sweet miniature paper envelope. Less than one song to go. And then Tyler will be . . . finished. He won't be satisfied, he can't summon the required sense of romance for that desperate hope, but he will have finished something, and it will exist in a world larger than the world of a living room wedding, or a few drinkers in a bar; it will be judged either harshly or generously, or ignored entirely, by people who do not know Tyler, who do not love Tyler, who don't give a shit about Tyler's past and present pains, who have no idea about taking him down, or rescuing him, or meeting him in California. It will go out into a crushing, cleansing indifference, but it will go out. It won't merely vanish, as completely as if it had never existed at all.

He'll find Liz, after he's finished. And he won't insist on going to the goddamned artichoke festival in Castroville, which (thank you, Google) is still six months away, anyway. That was just ironic, coffee-shop suavity, an attempt at perverse wit. He'll be happy, walking with Liz among redwood forests, watching eagles snatching fish from the deep-emerald surface of the Pacific. He'll be happy enough. That hope strikes him as reasonable.

Is that where the last song resides? Is it about a dream of redwoods and eagles; of a woman he could love ferociously, a woman with whom he could do erotic battle, a fantasy (who doesn't prefer fantasies to outcomes?) of aging-warrior love?

Or will that, too, be sentimental; will it be just another . . . song? Wishfulness about a woman walking among ancient trees, under a sky browsed by eagles. He can see, with dreadful clarity, how wrong it could go; how easily it might turn into another sad and familiar flight, the one about the woman in the woods, the peace and purity that waits, right over there, in a candlelit room, in another borough, on another coast . . .

But isn't the song entering the room, even now? There's a stir in the air. The trick, as Tyler has learned, is to act nonchalant, to lie in state on the sofa—his only earthly possession—like a sleeper waiting for the night's dreams to make themselves manifest.

Maybe—let's not rule it out—this will be the song that cuts clean, the one that matters, the one that sheds standard-issue romance and reveals, under its old skin, a raw blood-red devotion deeper than comfort, a desire profounder than schoolboy satisfaction, a yearning cold and immaculate and unstoppable as snow. Maybe it will be a lovingly sadistic slash, in lieu of wistful praise. Maybe it will be the wound that does not want healing; the search that knows it will never find the treasure but continues anyway, looking with ever-increasing diligence for that which cannot be discovered; understanding that it's the search that matters, not the first torch-lit glimpse of the buried chamber piled with gold and alabaster.

The dead, if the dead retain some vestige of consciousness, might feel alone in just this way—solitary, interred, as the world goes on without them. Barrett is somewhere, with Sam, and Tyler knows (he's been around long enough to know) that transubstantiation is occurring; that the inert consciouslessness of bread known, to Barrett, as Men has been summoned to life; that all those hours of ass-and-spine contact with the merciless wood of a pew were (surprise) leading somewhere, after all. Love, it would seem, has arrived. Or, maybe more accurately, Barrett has arrived at love. And he's done so with a man who'll carry him off; who will replace Tyler, as opposed to the series of hopeless affairs that (how long has Tyler known this?) were never meant to interfere—not in any serious or lasting way—with the brotherhood.

It's hardly ever the destination we've been anticipating, is it? Our hopes may seem unrealized, but we were in all likelihood hoping for the wrong thing. Where did we—the species, that is—pick up that strange and perverse habit?

Blessings on you, Barrett. From your older brother in a fourth-floor apartment on Avenue C. Not exactly an eye in the sky. But hey, we can only offer what we've got, right? Blessings from your slightly strung-out brother, who can't provide romance but can provide intimacy, and release. I know you. I've seen it. And, knowing all, I release you.

Heaven winked at you, right? Maybe. Maybe it did. Or maybe it was just an airplane and a cloud. But if Heaven winks at anybody, it's probably the less-than-conspicuous seekers; the ones who search among the discarded bits and pieces; the ones who choose the path over the avenue, the gap in the hedge over the trumpeted gates. That's probably why there's no verifiable evidence, right? The universe only winks at the ones no one will believe.

That's the joke? That's the joke inside the joke. Revelation is offered only to those too poor and obscure to be considered candidates.

From Tyler's position on the sofa, one of the two living room windows is perfectly centered between his feet. He can see the sprinkling of city lights through the window and, it seems, a lone star, a star so bright it can penetrate the New York sky. Or maybe it's an airplane. They take off from JFK and LaGuardia every ten minutes or so.

Tyler can't remember a time when he wasn't drawn to windows; when he didn't imagine he could take the leap, and not plummet but rise, until the constellations are closer than the streetlights.

You try singing your way closer to the stars (or even just the airplanes that impersonate stars), and the strange beauty of it is all wrapped up in their impossible remoteness, which would be true even if you *were* able to fly. Who'd want a proximate star? Who'd wish upon something reachable?

It's the song and it's the woman. It's the song you can imagine, but can't quite sing. Same goes for the woman.

Or is that just more romantic crap?

Liz herself is, or soon will be, a light in the sky, as she, along with a host of others, flies west from JFK. Is she, even now, right now, up there in the night sky, looking down at the lights of New York City? Is she thinking of Tyler (at ten thousand feet, and still climbing) as Tyler thinks of her?

Thinking of Liz, thinking of stars and airplane lights in a nocturnal sky, Tyler is suddenly sure of it: Liz is looking down at him just as he's looking up at her, through the ceiling, through the three other apartments piled on top of his, where other people, unknown to him, strive and hope and wonder; ask themselves how, exactly, they seem to have ended up here; debate about whether to mention the paucity of the larder, the extravagance of the bed linens (600-count Egyptian cotton, what even *is* that?), or just, you know, see what's on TV tonight.

There's that speck in his eye again. He rubs at it, but it remains lodged against his retina.

It occurs to him: he's had something in his eye for quite a while now. He's merely more aware of it at certain times than he is at others.

An unbidden flash of recognition (wow, an old one): that ice crystal that blew into the bedroom—how long ago? When Beth was dying for the first time; when Tyler got out of bed and closed the window; when he was so sure he'd be able to take care of everything, of everyone . . .

Has it been lodged in his eye since then?

No. That's crazy. Tyler is lost in a mist of suggestibility. Which is where he most wants to be.

He has done what's been asked of him. He's loved others to the best of his ability. He's seen his brother delivered; he's made good on the vow he made, long ago, to the apparition that claimed to be his mother.

What if that were enough? What if the last song needs to remain unfinished; what if Tyler, by continuing to strive, can only botch it? What if the window is telling him, by so perfectly positioning itself smack between his splayed feet, that it's time to fly?

Tyler can't quite tell whether he's getting up off the sofa, or merely speculating about it.

Still—maybe it's been summoned by the haunted sofa, by the window, by the short distance that lies between them—it seems that something—something—has entered the room; something that's about to lay a note on Tyler's forehead, soft as a good-night kiss. It's about to give him this last song, this parting gift, this rose that will start wilting the moment it's laid on his pillow. It's going to be a lament for Beth, married to a love song for Liz. It's going to insinuate itself into his tired brain (that circus monkey, insisting it can play a sonata on a miniature concertina), and then—because it's the last and most glorious disappointment, the unreachable destination, the woman who will always leave—it's going to set him free. After that, the stars might slip a wink to Tyler, too. Once he's finished the song, and become invisible again. Then he can answer what the window asks, about staying in the room, or taking flight.

He remains where he is, prone, supplicant, waiting. He thinks of Liz, the lights of her aircraft, high above him. Liz, it would seem, has joined the sky.

He says, or imagines saying, Hey Goddess. Are you there?

ACKNOWLEDGMENTS

I can't imagine my life as a writer without the twenty-five years of insight, input, and encouragement I've received from Ken Corbett.

Gail Hochman, my agent; Jonathan Galassi, my editor; and I have been a virtual literary SWAT team for more years than I (or, I suspect, they) care to remember. I'm grateful as well to Marianne Merola, who takes such scrupulous care of any and all foreign editions.

Part of this book was written at Beatrice von Rezzori's Santa Maddalena Foundation. Beatrice's generosity and friendship have been significant aspects of my life for over a decade.

I'm particularly thankful to Marie Howe, who can spot an off-kilter phrase the way a hawk can spot a mouse from five hundred feet in the air. Other vital readers include Frances Coady, Jessie Gaynor, Daniel Kaizer, James Lecesne, Christian McCulloch, Adam Moss, Christopher Potter, Seth Pybas, Sal Randolph, and Derrick Smit.

Jonathan Parks-Ramage, Jessie Gaynor, and Fiona True kept me going, in various ways, throughout the writing of this book. Jochen Hartmann informed me about the Bushwick of the years 2004 through 2008.

I was reminded weekly about readers' capacities for thought, and their sensitivities to nuance, by Tim Berry, Jen Cabral, Billy Hough, Dan Minahan, Nina West, and Ann Wood. In addition, as I was trying to better understand the songwriting process, Billy actually came over to my house with an electric piano, to teach me about the differences between a major and a minor chord.

David Hopson's visual sense is inspiring.

The copy editor, John McGhee, not only caught every grammatical lapse and inconsistency of usage, but noted certain phrases I had unwittingly used as many as eight or nine times.

Miranda Popkey and Christopher Richards turned a stack of dog-eared, stained pages into a book.

Thanks as well to Steven Barclay, Michael Warner, and Sally Wilcox.

And, finally, this book would not exist (for reasons known to them) without Billy Hough, Tracy McPartland, and Nina West.